Dan listened ~~to~~
sleeping pea~~cefully~~

Last night had been ~~special~~. All this time, he'd
thought he could find someone who just wanted to
have sex, and that would be that. The terrible truth
was that he hadn't had sex with Annie. He'd made
love. *Love.* The last thing he needed.

Damn it. This wasn't supposed to happen.

If he left now, no one would be hurt. But he wanted
to be there when she woke up. *He wanted to make
love to her again….*

He dared another look, knowing it was a mistake.
Lord, she was beautiful. Her hair was tousled and
sexy. The sheet covered her only to the waist, and
his gaze wandered over her body. Perfect. Just
perfect. Her breasts weren't very large, but they
suited her. They suited him.

Sighing, he crept out of bed. Annie stirred and
opened her eyes.

"Dan, did I say thanks?" She smiled up at him.

"Yeah, honey. You did."

"Good." Closing her eyes, she drifted off once more.

Dan moved away, and suddenly stepped on
something on the carpet. Bending, he picked up
the object. His chest clenched. "Damn it," he
whispered. It was a tiny pink shoe. The kind that
fitted a Barbie doll.

Dear Reader,

I was absolutely thrilled at the opportunity to write a book for the TEXAS MEN miniseries, mostly because I had so many of my own experiences to draw from when I created Dan and Annie. You see, about two years ago I met the man of my dreams from an ad. It wasn't *Texas Men* magazine, but it was close. It was a Texas Internet dating service. I was just as nervous as Annie when I sent out my first reply. And just like Annie, when I became brave enough to meet my mystery man in person, I knew I'd found my heart's desire.

So not only did I enjoy writing about Dan and Annie, but as you'll see, one of my leading characters in the book is none other than Barbie! Yep, the same Barbie I played with as a young girl, the one with the dream house and the even dreamier Ken. I've since discovered that many, many women share fond and lasting memories of Barbie. She was as big a part of our childhood as Harlequin romance novels were a part of our young adulthood.

I hope this book rekindles some romantic memories for you, and that Dan and Annie's story makes you remember the day you fell head over heels in love.

All my best,

Jo Leigh

P.S. Don't forget to look for my next book, #749 *If Wishes Were...Daddies,* A Harlequin American Romance novel available in November 1998.

Jo Leigh
SINGLE SHERIFF SEEKS...

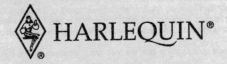

HARLEQUIN®

TORONTO • NEW YORK • LONDON
AMSTERDAM • PARIS • SYDNEY • HAMBURG
STOCKHOLM • ATHENS • TOKYO • MILAN • MADRID
PRAGUE • WARSAW • BUDAPEST • AUCKLAND

To my wonderful friends Christina Dodd
and Heather MacAllister, whose creativity made this
book come to life.
I owe you guys.

ISBN 0-373-25799-6

SINGLE SHERIFF SEEKS...

Copyright © 1998 by Jolie Kramer.

Printed in U.S.A.

Prologue

JESSIE HIGGINS took one last look down the hall before she closed the door to the conference room. Sheriff Dan Collins was all the way out at the Fisher place, but it didn't hurt to be careful. No sense in spoiling the whole plan now. The middle-aged dispatcher turned to the coffeepot on the credenza and waited while Logan finished putting the cream in his cup. Once everyone had their drinks and doughnuts, the meeting could begin. Frankly, she couldn't wait. This was the most excitement she'd had in years.

"All right, people," Reese Collins said. "Let's settle. We don't have much time." He grinned. "I now call the Project Dan Committee to order."

Jessie laughed with the others, then poured a cup of strong coffee for herself. By the time she'd taken her seat next to Frank and Kirstie Collins, everyone looked ready to get to work. She waved her hand. "Margaret came up with something," she said. Jessie looked over at her fellow dispatcher. "Go ahead, Margaret. Tell them."

The older woman, a sheriff's dispatcher for over twenty years, looked down shyly for a moment, then smiled. "Barbie," she said.

"What?" Reese leaned forward, and all of the deputies except Sandy Kellog did too.

"Barbie," Margaret said. "You know, the doll."

"What about it?"

"I've got three. Sandy there has two. Gina Painter has one worth about two thousand dollars, isn't that right, Jessie?"

Jessie nodded. "Yep. Between us all, we have close to a hundred thousand dollars' worth of collectible Barbies right here in Harlen."

Reese laughed. "My poor brother's gonna blow a gasket."

"But it'll work," Margaret said.

"That it will. Now what about finding the next Mrs. Collins?"

"I've got that covered."

All eyes went to Mike Thomas. The deputy brought out a slick oversize magazine. He held it up, and Jessie saw the title: *Texas Men.*

"This is for ads. Personal ads. It's all about men just like Dan. I figure we write the ad, we screen the candidates, we make the deal. Simple."

"We'll need to work on the ad some," Kirstie said. She looked at Reese. "Our brother is mighty particular. We sure don't want to find someone like Melissa."

"So you be in charge of that," Reese said. "But we need to move fast. He's getting worse. Yesterday I thought he was going to put a bullet through that old dishwasher of his."

Eleven heads nodded. They all knew that the

Dan Situation was getting more serious every day. There was only one solution: Dan Collins was going to fall in love—whether he liked it or not. The whole damn town was going to see to it.

ANNIE JONES wanted to throttle her little sister. But since Rachel was two inches taller and a lot stronger, she held back.

"I'm not going unless you go," Rachel said stubbornly. "Period. So you'd better pack your bags, Annie, because you're going to Harlen."

"You manipulative little b—"

"Annie!" Rachel rose from the couch, smiling in victory. "Such language. You ought to be ashamed."

"I don't like this," she said.

"You don't like anything new."

"That's not true."

"Oh, yeah? You're talking to me now, not one of your adoring little students. I know better."

Annie walked over to the kitchen table and looked down at the magazine Rachel had brought with her. "But answering an ad from a magazine? Come on, Rachel. This is weird, even for you."

"If you'd take a minute and read the ad, instead of dismissing it out of hand, maybe you'd see my point."

Annie sighed. It was crucial that Rachel take the summer job Annie had gotten her. It would keep her sister out of trouble, give her something constructive to do, and best of all, if she could stick it out, it would provide her with her tuition for the next two semesters. More than that, it could give her some confidence. A way to feel better about herself after the awful year she'd just been through.

But because Rachel was Rachel, Annie was going to have to agree to this ridiculous bargain. She sat down and looked at the picture of the man Rachel had chosen for her. A sheriff. His name was Dan Collins. At thirty-two he was five years older than she was. Nice-looking, if you went for guys in uniform. His hair was a little shorter than she liked, but then she was used to university types who avoid barbers the way Superman avoids kryptonite. But there was something kind in his eyes. Or maybe that was a trick of the light.

"Well? Are you going to read it or not?"

"Give me a second, would you?"

"If you don't, I'll read it for you."

Annie turned. "I think there's some Häagen Dazs in the freezer. Rum Raisin."

Rachel's eyes widened, and she hurried to the kitchen. Annie smiled. It worked every time.

Now that she was left alone for a moment, she read the ad.

Single Sheriff Seeks...

Hi, I'm Dan Collins. I'm the sheriff here in Harlen, Texas, a little town just outside of

Houston. I'm divorced, 32, college-educated, and healthy. I'm looking for a woman who's got common sense, a good sense of humor, and who likes the pace of small-town living. Pretty isn't as important as nice.

Well, she had to admit the ad wasn't what she expected. Especially that last line. Although Annie didn't consider herself ugly, she was no beauty queen, either. And nice was more important than handsome in her book, too.

"Well?" Rachel stood beside the table, the pint of ice cream in one hand, and a tablespoon in the other. "Didn't I tell you?"

"What am I supposed to do in Harlen for two months?"

"I told you. They're looking for someone to teach art classes at the YMCA. It's perfect. You know darn well you've always wanted to see what living in a small town is like. Now's your chance." Rachel sat down and concentrated on her dessert for a moment.

Annie took the time to look at her. Really look at her. She was the pretty one. Today her long, dark hair was held back by a headband, which was particularly becoming. It showed off her large green eyes, great cheekbones and perfect, full lips. It was hard to love a face like that, even when it belonged to your sister. But Annie did. She loved Rachel with all her heart, and despite the fact that she'd gotten all the looks in the family, Annie was sure if she could just settle down for a bit, Rachel could find the happiness she deserved.

Besides, Rachel was right about one thing. Annie had always had a thing about small-town living. It was probably romantic nonsense, but the idea of knowing her neighbors, not having to lock her doors at night, and an ice-cream parlor where everyone went on a balmy Saturday night was her idea of heaven. She took a deep breath. "All right."

Rachel froze with the spoon in her mouth. "Wrewwy?"

"Really."

Her sister took the spoon out, shoved it into the ice cream and leapt to her feet. Before she knew what hit her, Annie was in her arms, being hugged half to death.

She waited a minute before she broke the embrace. "I'm just going to meet the man. Once. That's all."

"Twice," Rachel said. "Or no deal."

"No fair."

"I never said I was going to be fair. Anyway, that's what I told him in the letter."

"What letter?" Annie felt a panicky flutter in her chest. "Don't tell me you already answered this ad!"

Rachel nodded. "I couldn't let him get away. He's perfect."

"It's an *ad* for heaven's sake! How do you know it's not all made up?"

"Because I talked with his sister."

"You *what*?"

"I spoke to his sister. She assured me that the ad wasn't nearly as great as the guy. If he's half as nice as his sister, you're going to fall for him in a minute."

"Rachel, you kill me. Don't you know yet that things like that just don't happen outside of the movies? The odds of the two of us even liking each other are way off the map. The whole idea is crazy."

"It is not. It's just as logical as any other way to meet a guy."

"Who said I wanted to meet a guy in the first place?"

"You can't tell me you like being alone. Come on, Annie. It's me you're talking to." Rachel put her hands on Annie's shoulders and looked her in the eyes. "I'd never let you go if I didn't think these were straight-up, good people. You might not fall in love, but you'll make some new friends, and you'll get to live part of your dream. What's so terrible about that?"

Annie stared back at her. It wasn't easy to admit it, but Rachel was right. She had no other plans for the summer. The town of Harlen seemed like the kind of place she'd longed for. She would only have to meet this sheriff twice. How bad could it be?

One more time, she said, "All right. But this means that no matter what, you're sticking with that job until school starts."

"Yes, ma'am," Rachel agreed.

"I have a bad feeling about this," Annie said, looking once more at the man in the magazine. "An awfully bad feeling."

"Piffle," Rachel said. "This summer is going to change your life, Annie Jones. I guarantee it."

"I just hope it changes it for the better."

2

DAN COLLINS didn't want to go to the damn barbecue. He didn't want to drink lemonade. Eat ribs. Throw a Frisbee. Talk to his family. Smile. He didn't even feel like being civil. What he wanted to do was go home. Turn on ESPN. Have a beer. Pet his dog. Mostly, what he wanted was to be left alone.

Fat chance.

That was the trouble with small towns. Every damn body knew every damn thing about every other damn body. He should move. Houston wasn't far. Big old city like that, a man could get lost. Have a private thought. Big city like that, no one would give a spit if a guy was in a bad mood every once in a while.

Dan toyed with the notion of going home. Really doing it, instead of just thinking about it. But he knew he wouldn't. Trouble with him was, he was too soft. His sister Kirstie would be all upset if he didn't show. Then his brother Reese would call. Shortly after that, Frank would get on the horn, and before he knew it, Mom would be calling him Daniel and he'd feel like the scum of the earth. All over a barbecue.

Well, he'd go. But he wouldn't have a good time.

He put the patrol car in gear and headed down the drive, leaving the new municipal building behind. It still didn't feel like his department. He'd grown used to the old place. Sure, he'd complained about the air conditioning, the leaky water heater and the lousy wiring, but it had been home to the sheriff's department since before his daddy could remember. There was a history to the old building. This new place, white and sterile and perfectly cooled, was too modern. It didn't fit the town and it didn't fit him.

As he drove down Main, he checked out both sides of the street. Just habit. Nothing of a criminal nature was going on. Oh, maybe there was a library book past due sitting on the counter at the Green Shade diner, but that would be about it. Not much for a sheriff to do in this little speck of a town. Except go to damn barbecues.

It didn't take long to get to Reese's. Six minutes. Already there were trucks and cars lining the streets by his house. Half the town would be there. Shaking hands and kissing cheeks like they hadn't seen each other every day for the last hundred years. He parked, grumbling, got out, put on his hat, pushed up his sleeves and headed on in. They probably didn't even have any Coors.

"Uncle Dan!"

He heard Cory a split second before the five-year-old tackled his knees. It was tricky keeping his balance, but he did, then he turned and scooped the boy up in his arms. Cory was giggling before Dan could start tickling him. It was a lot like holding on to a big old speckled trout, the way he wiggled.

"So at least someone can get a smile out of you these days."

He didn't acknowledge his sister's sarcasm. Instead, he found the spot on his nephew's chest that produced the most laughter.

"When you're finished, you can bring that wiggle worm out to the backyard. I heard a rumor that someone wanted to play some catch."

Cory's struggles changed. He wanted down, and Dan eased him to the ground. Without a backward glance, the boy was off, running through the house with complete disregard for life, limb or furniture. Dan looked over at Kirstie. Arms folded across her chest, she stared at him with curious interest.

"What?" he asked. "I'm here, aren't I?"

"I feel so honored."

"Come on, Kirstie. Don't start up."

She approached him, walking around the leather couch in their brother's spacious living room. Funny thing about Kirstie. She just kept getting prettier. Twenty-seven years old, tall, slim, her long dark hair the exact same shade as his own, she constantly surprised him with her looks. When he wasn't with her, he thought of her as his kid sister. Wearing jeans and old T-shirts, ragged sneakers, any baseball cap she could beg, borrow or steal. She was a pip-squeak, a pest. Someone who insisted on tagging along to the park or the baseball diamond. Not this grown-up woman who wore makeup and worked the news desk at the Harlen *Tribune.*

"Are you going to be sullen the entire afternoon?" she asked. "Or can you get over yourself long enough to be pleasant to our neighbors?"

"Get over myself?"

"If your moods aren't the supreme act of self-indulgence, I don't know what is. Male posturing at its worst."

"Did you read another book? *Men Are Jerks From Pluto* or something?"

She made a face. "I don't need a book to figure out what's got your butt bent out of shape."

"No?"

"You, dear brother, are suffering from an acute case of celibacy."

"What?"

"Celibacy. It means—"

"I know what it means," he said, inching toward the back door and escape. "And you sure as hell better know what it means, too."

She laughed. "You're so cute when you're reactionary."

"Reactionary, my—where's the beer? Did he get Coors?"

"The beer is where it's supposed to be, but don't change the subject."

"I was never on the subject." He slid open the sliding glass door that led to the backyard. "Now go find Frank and bug him for a while. I'm thirsty."

"Wait. I'll come with you. There's someone I want you to meet."

"I don't want to meet any of your friends, Kirstie. I'm serious."

She met him at the door and looked up. Her blithe smile told him she didn't particularly care what he wanted. "Her name is Annie. Annie Jones. And she's not my friend. Well, not yet anyway."

"So why would I want to meet her?"

"For one thing, she's your new neighbor. Or didn't you notice the moving van?"

He had, but he hadn't given it a moment's thought. "What's the other thing?"

The blithe smile turned enigmatic. "You'll see."

He didn't like the sound of that. But Kirstie grabbed him by the arm and pulled him behind her as she joined the thirty or so folks standing around the huge yard. Even though it wasn't even noon yet, the heat was palpable, making that beer sound even better. The smells of hamburgers, hot dogs, barbecue sauce and charcoal hit him squarely, and his stomach grumbled in appreciation. He hadn't eaten breakfast. Lately he was always forgetting to eat.

The beer cooler was right next to the picnic tables, and he broke free from Kirstie's grasp to head in that direction. Whatever her second reason was for introducing him to this woman, it would go down better with a cold one. The path to liquid refreshment wasn't an easy one, though. He kept getting stopped. People kept smiling at him, asking him how he was. But it was peculiar, somehow. Not the normal "Hey, how are ya?" kind of talk.

Sylvia Trainer touched his arm, stared at him hard and said, "Why hello, Sheriff."

"Hey."

"How *are* you?"

He shrugged, baffled. Sylvia wasn't exactly a bosom buddy. He knew her from school, but she was Reese's friend. As far as he knew, she'd never given a damn how he was before. Why now?

"Can I get you a burger?" she asked. "I brought potato salad. Your favorite."

"No, that's okay." This was getting weird.

She smiled at him, the same way Kirstie had. "All right," she said, with great significance. "We'll talk later." Then she wiggled her eyebrows.

"Sure," he said. He had no idea why he'd want to talk to her later. Or why everyone within earshot was looking at him so carefully. So surreptitiously. It wasn't his birthday, so this couldn't be a surprise party. He zeroed in on the beer cooler. That, at least, he understood.

He finally made it unmolested, and bent down to pick up a tall-necked bottle. As he stood, he saw that his brothers, Reese, Ted and Frank, had come up behind him. He twisted the cap off his beer and took a long drink before giving them a nod.

"Dan," Ted said, his voice a low monotone that had scared junior-high-school students for the better part of ten years.

"What's up?" Dan took another swig and looked from brother to brother. Something was going on, all right. All three of them were giving him the once-over. "Why the looks? What the hell's going on with everybody today?"

"What do you mean?" Reese bent for a beer of his own. When he straightened, his expression was neutral. But then Reese was a politician. He was good at putting on masks.

"Cut the crap, Reese. Tell me."

Reese glanced at Frank and Ted, then behind him. As one, the three brothers moved aside. It was like a curtain opening, but Dan didn't see anything special. Just Kirstie. And someone he didn't know, whose back was to him.

The rear view wasn't half-bad, though. She was in jeans. Very nicely in jeans. She curved just the way a woman is supposed to curve. Slim at the waist, rounder at the hips. Long legs. He dragged his gaze up enough to notice how her pale blond hair fell to the middle of her back. Even from here it looked shiny and soft. He hadn't even seen her face, yet he felt a tug in his groin. Maybe Kirstie hadn't been so off the mark with that celibacy crack. He hadn't gone out with a woman since Melissa had left him almost two years ago. It wasn't natural, that much he knew. But surprisingly, it hadn't been that difficult. No one in Harlen interested him that way. And he hadn't left Harlen.

Now there was this new neighbor. Annie Jones. Annie Jones with the very nice-fitting jeans. Was it possible that his long dry spell could be over? He sipped his beer again and tried to remember sex. Ah, yes. That was it. It wasn't all that hard to recall. He had the feeling if Ms. Jones's front was half as nice as her back, his memory was soon going to be nearly photographic.

He waited another tense moment, and then she turned. Okay. Bingo. All on alert and full speed ahead. The woman was a knockout. An eleven. Maybe a twelve. His body, which had been dormant for these many months, suddenly woke up. In an instant, it responded like a spaniel pointing out a flock of quails.

Dan needed to leave. Now. Damn it, she was walking toward him. How charming to meet her under these circumstances. He could hear Kirstie's introduction now. "Annie, I'd like you to meet my brother, the pervert."

He turned quickly and started walking toward the house. In desperation, he started thinking of baseball scores. National league stats. RBIs. Anything that had nothing whatsoever to do with sex.

It wasn't working, though. Why in hell didn't Reese have a swimming pool?

"Dan!"

He heard Kirstie's shout, but he ignored it. It wasn't that he wanted to be rude, but there was no possible way he was going to meet that woman while he was in this state.

Ducking inside the house, he made a beeline for the stairs to the basement. No one would be there. He could calm down, get back to being himself. The cool dark of the playroom would be just the ticket.

The door was open, and he hurried down. Alone at last, he sighed deeply, then took a long, slow sip of beer. There. That did it. He was in control again. Back to being Dan, not some randy teenager.

What the hell was going on? He couldn't remember a single time since he'd gotten past puberty when something like this had happened to him. Not with Melissa. Not with anyone. He didn't even know this woman Annie, for pity's sake. Maybe he was sick, like with the flu, only the symptoms of this disease were a lot more humiliating. It had nothing to do with the woman. She had just been in his line of sight when he'd been whammied.

He heard someone on the steps, and he froze. When he looked up, he saw it was Kirstie. And she was alone.

"What was that about?" she asked. "Why'd you run off like that? I can't believe you."

"It was an emergency."

She got to the landing and strode toward him angrily. "A rudeness emergency?"

"I didn't mean to be rude. I'm sorry."

She glared for a moment. "So come on back up and meet her. I'm sure she thinks you're nuts, but maybe there's a chance you can change her mind."

"I don't think so."

"What?"

"I don't think so. But thanks."

"Uh-uh. No way. You're not going to embarrass me like that."

"Embarrass you? Why would it embarrass you?"

"Because I've told her you want to meet her. Because she's a nice lady, and I think we're going to be friends, and I don't want her thinking I have a jerk for a brother."

"Ah. Well, just tell her I don't feel well. I'll sneak out. No one will be the wiser."

"No! You're not going. I insist you meet her. I'm not kidding, Dan. Don't make me call Mom."

"Mom?" He laughed. Some things never changed. "Mom isn't going to make me change my mind. I don't want to meet Annie Jones, okay? Deal with it."

"It's all right. You don't have to."

Dan spun toward the stairs, bumping into Kirstie as he moved. Annie Jones. On the fifth step. The light was behind her, so he couldn't make out her features. Instead, he saw a halo of golden hair. A slim, tall vision of beauty. He tried to think of something to say. Nothing came.

"Annie, this is my brother," Kirstie said. "Despite all appearances, he really can be a decent sort of person."

Annie walked down the rest of the stairs and approached him slowly. Now he could see her face, and it was just as lovely as he'd imagined. Pale skin, big green eyes, pink lips. But more than the features, what drew him in was the look in her eyes. The humor, the gentleness.

Kirstie nudged him hard in the side with her elbow, and he saw that Annie was holding her hand out to be shaken. He took it, and when they touched he felt that stir again. This time, however, he didn't humiliate himself completely. He concentrated on his actions, on the room, on the beer in his other hand, and managed to keep himself together.

"It's a pleasure to meet you," Annie said.

"You too. I'm sorry I seemed rude outside. It hasn't been a particularly good day."

"Understood." She looked at him for a while, then her gaze shifted down.

To their hands. He hadn't let her go. He did so, immediately. She just gave him the nicest smile. Sweet, real sweet.

"So you're the sheriff," she said.

He nodded, watching the way her lips fell right back into the little grin. Like the Mona Lisa.

"Annie is a teacher," Kirstie said, giving him another jab in the side.

He tore his gaze from her mouth. Damn it. He really must have the flu. This was nuts. "What kind of a teacher?"

"I was teaching sociology at Baylor. But I'm off for summer vacation."

"Why are you here?"

"Dan!" Kirstie jabbed him again. He was gonna have a doozy of a bruise tomorrow. "What he meant to say was, welcome to Harlen. Hope you like it here. It's a nice town, with nice people. Isn't that right, Dan?"

He nodded guiltily. "Look, I wasn't kidding about this being a rotten day. I'm sorry. I do hope you'll like it here. But I've got to go."

Annie nodded. "Sure. No problem. I hope things improve."

He backed up, not trusting himself to pass too close to her. The backs of his legs hit a leather ottoman, and he lost his balance. He sat down, hard, spilling the rest of his beer.

Kirstie burst out laughing. Annie had the good manners to try and hold back, although he could see she was having trouble. He felt his cheeks heat. Another first. He'd never blushed in his whole damn life.

Then Annie turned to Kirstie. "I'd love to meet the rest of your family."

Kirstie stopped laughing long enough to say, "Sure."

Annie started up the stairs. He'd never been more grateful. The woman had the decency to ignore him. To pretend he hadn't just made the biggest fool of himself in the western world. That he wasn't sitting on a stool, blushing like a schoolgirl.

Kirstie, on the other hand, kept right on laughing. Just as the two of them reached the top of the stairs, he heard her say, "I know you won't believe me, but he's really not a geek. Honest."

A geek. Great. So much for a good first impression.

3

ANNIE WALKED into her new apartment and almost turned right around and walked out again. It was crammed with a mass of boxes, all in a clump, sitting in the living room. The work ahead of her held no appeal, especially after the way she'd overeaten at the barbecue.

Picking her way through the clutter, she went to the kitchen and gave thanks that she'd had the sense to put some cold sodas on ice. Just hearing the fizz as she popped open the top made her feel better. No glasses were unpacked yet, so she took the can and went straight to the bedroom. It was sparsely furnished—only a queen-size bed, a dresser and a small writing desk—but it was cool and it didn't shout "Get to work" at her quite as loudly as the living room.

Luckily, the bed was nice and solid, but soft where it needed to be. She curled her legs under her, looked out the window, and thought about her second day in Harlen. What an introduction to small-town life.

Kirstie had been a wonderful hostess, and Annie thought there was a real chance they could be friends. She wasn't so sure about the rest of the townspeople. They'd certainly taken an interest in her. Everywhere she'd looked, people stared, quite shamelessly. Kirstie had said it was normal, nothing to worry about. She was the new kid in town, after all. But something had seemed a little unnerving to Annie. People knew too much about her. Her name. That she was going to be teaching at the Y. Where she was living. Talk about a grapevine. When she'd imagined living in a small town, she had dreamed of good neighbors, but this was ridiculous.

Then, of course, there had been that meeting with Dan Collins. She still wasn't sure what that had been about. It had stayed with her all afternoon.

She'd been surprised by her reaction to him. His picture didn't do him justice. He was a tall, dynamic man, with a power that had been evident at first glance. His body, muscled in a natural, unselfconscious way, had almost vibrated with health and strength. Maybe it was his hand that had cemented that image—so large it could have crushed hers in a heartbeat, but gentle, too. As if he knew that with a simple handshake he had the power to hurt her, so he mustn't squeeze too hard.

Or it could have been the set of his jaw. His face was an interesting combination of sharp angles and surprising softness. He'd tried to appear gruff—she could see that right away—but there was an openness in his gaze that no amount of surliness could have hidden. Although he'd kept his lips tightly together, it was a natural smile he was trying to keep at bay.

So, it hadn't been the disaster she'd imagined. At least from her end. The way he'd bolted from the party, it was pretty clear that she hadn't met his expectations. That's the way it always seemed to go, though. At least for her. If she was interested, the guy wasn't. And the guys who were interested didn't do a darn thing for her.

She scooted off the bed. She wasn't really interested in Dan Collins. His looks were great, no doubt about that, but, thank goodness, she'd gotten past that as a criterion long ago. Three things mattered to her in a man. Smarts, humor, and kindness. Mostly kindness. Funny how that had become a rare commodity these days. Good looks were way down on the list, right below cooking skills and the ability to fix cars.

It would have been kind of nice, though, to strike up a friendship with a man like him. She'd wager it wasn't only his face that held surprises. There was something going on with the long, tall cowboy. Something intriguing.

She'd dawdled long enough. It was time to unpack. First the bedroom, so when she collapsed she could do so under her comforter.

The living room mess hadn't gotten any neater, so she put her soda down and started with the top box. As she worked, her mind kept returning to Dan.

Kirstie had told her not to mention the ad in *Texas Men*. Dan was shy, she'd said. That added another piece to the puzzle. Several times, his name had come up in other conversations. He used to go on the rodeo circuit, but he hadn't done that for a few years. He was clearly well liked as a sheriff. And his family was a close one. Someone had said something about his ex-wife, reminding her that the ad had mentioned he was divorced.

Lots of little clues to play with. As she carried her sheets to the linen closet, she remembered the look on his face when he'd lost his balance. Of all the clues, that was the biggest. He'd blushed and stammered and, frankly, that's what had made her regretful that she wouldn't get to know that guy. That cute, vulnerable, kind of bumbling he-man. She'd always preferred Clark Kent to Superman.

Oh well. Better not to dwell on it. She'd fulfilled half of her promise to Rachel. One more meeting to go, and she could forget all about Clark.

DAN LISTENED carefully. He'd been listening for the past two hours. The walls in his building weren't thick enough to insulate him from the sounds in the next apartment, especially when he sat on the couch against the shared living-room wall. She'd been busy, that's for sure. Unpacking, no doubt. He'd toyed with the notion of offering to help, but discarded it shortly after his second beer.

He was not going to get involved in one of Kirstie's matchmaking schemes. Sure, Annie was a pretty thing. Big deal. There were lots of pretty women. He wasn't going to let himself get all bent out of shape about it. Ugly things had a way of turning up inside beautiful packages.

He'd already made peace with his physical reaction to her. That celibacy idea wasn't too far off the mark. He remembered quite clearly the last time he'd been with a woman. Melissa. It wasn't a good memory. Remembering had kept him on the straight and narrow for a long time. Maybe too long.

There had been offers. Good offers. He just hadn't been ready. This afternoon had been a pretty big sign that things had changed. It was time to get out there again. Make an appearance at the Jerky Fiddle. Maybe give Wanda a call.

A loud crash from next door made him wince. It was a big one. No teacup, that's for sure. Cougar, his black Lab, got up from his nap and came over to the couch. Dan rubbed his ears and listened. No more crashes. Maybe he should go on over there and lend her a hand. It was the neighborly thing to do. Besides, she might be hurt. Maybe she'd cut herself on whatever it was that broke.

He stood, and ran a quick hand through his hair, then down his chin. The stubble there scratched him, and he thought about shaving. But only for a second. He was just going to help the lady move a few boxes, not take her out on a date.

Shaking his head over his own foolishness, he left his apartment and walked the few steps to her door. He hesitated, but only until he heard another bump. Nothing broke that time, at least. He knocked.

Several seconds went by. He didn't knock again, though. If she didn't answer soon, he'd just slip back home.

The door opened. She stared up at him in surprise. Her hair was a mess. She'd piled it on top of her head, but most of it had come loose. Her shirt was half-untucked from her pants. Somehow she'd managed to rip her jeans, a good long tear on her right thigh. And yep, she'd hurt herself. A bandage was wrapped around her left foot.

His gaze moved back up, slowly, and when he reached her face once more, he realized he wasn't breathing. He took in a big gulp of air and let it out, but it was too late. His heart was beating like a jackhammer.

"Hello," Annie said, swatting loose hair away from her face. "Can I help you?"

He shook his head. "That's what I came to ask you."

She looked puzzled.

He pointed to her bandage. "You got hurt."

She lifted her bare foot and wiggled her toes. Her red-painted toes.

"It's nothing. Just a little piece of glass. I broke a serving dish. Stupid, I know, but I tripped."

"Shouldn't do this kinda work barefoot."

She wrinkled her nose. Her very cute nose. "Shoes. If I had my way, I'd never wear them."

"Not very sensible, if you ask me."

Her eyes widened. She started to say something, but obviously thought better of it. Finally, she said, "Thanks for your offer, but I've got everything under control."

Stupid. Stupid and rude, and damn it, he hadn't even meant it. Damn. "I didn't mean... You look like a real sensible girl."

She smiled a little. "Thanks. I think. But really, I've just got a few more boxes to unpack. I'll be fine."

He should go. She wanted him to go. He had no reason to stay. She was just another of Kirstie's attempts at getting him married again, which he wasn't about to do. "I'd better look at that foot," he said. And then he took a step inside.

Annie looked surprised. Hell, *he* was surprised. It wasn't like him to butt in where he wasn't wanted. But someone had to make sure she wasn't going to get an infection in that foot.

"Make yourself at home," she said, although he didn't believe she meant it.

He'd just take a look. One look. Then he was out of here. He moved quickly to the couch, sat down, and patted his knee. "Come on," he said.

"Come on what?"

"Put your foot up here. I can't look at it if you're standing on it."

"Are you also the town doctor?" she asked.

"I've mended a few broken bones, but no. We have a doctor on Main Street." He patted his knee again. "Well?"

She looked at him kind of funny, as if she couldn't figure out if he was trying to be helpful, or if he just had a foot fetish. That made him smile. Up until today, he'd never thought one way or another about feet. But those red toes. He could get in trouble by thinking too long about them. "I'm not going to bite you," he said.

She sighed, then she limped over to stand in front of him. Balancing on her good foot, she put the wounded one on his knee. He touched her, lightly, but she teetered and almost fell.

"Come on over here," he said, indicating the other side of the couch. "Sit down, and then we'll try it again."

"I don't think this is necessary," she said. "It was only a tiny piece of glass."

"You put anything on it?"

She shook her head.

He grunted. "You got anything to put on it?"

She nodded.

"Well?"

She seemed startled. "Oh, okay. I'll just be a minute." Then she hobbled toward the bathroom, but the funny thing was, she looked back at him three times. Each time, her expression was more puzzled than the last.

For some reason, that made him grin. She was confused by him. Him. Straight-talking, sure-footed Dan Collins. He hadn't confused a woman in a long, long time.

While she was gone, he took a look around the place. She'd done a lot. Only a few boxes were still waiting to be unpacked. He noticed a few pictures on the mantelpiece. One of her parents, at least that's what he assumed. Another of Annie standing with a real pretty girl who had the same nose, the same eyes. Her sister, he'd wager. No others. No men.

She came back, then, holding a spray bottle of antiseptic. She hesitated a bit as she neared the couch, but then she sat, angling herself so she could comfortably put her foot on his knee.

Dan took the bottle, then waited for her to settle. Her heel dug into his thigh a little. Not enough to hurt, just enough to make him very aware.

He started to unwrap her foot. It was impossible not to touch her bare skin, even though he tried. Right away he knew it had been a mistake to insist. He was feeling a pressure he shouldn't be feeling. Not when he was just being neighborly. Hell, maybe he did have a foot fetish, and he just hadn't known it.

Swallowing hard, he finished unwrapping. He couldn't get a good look at the wound without moving her foot. Which would mean touching it again. His hand came down, and the minute he made contact, the pressure in his jeans became urgent. He could feel his cheeks heat up. His breathing get all raggedy. It was time to leave.

He pulled her foot back, took a cursory glance at the very small puncture and grabbed the spray antiseptic. He swallowed again as he doused her foot, then quickly wrapped her foot right back up. It wasn't a very pretty job, but it would do.

He figured she'd move her foot right away. But she didn't. She just kept it there. On his thigh. Only a few inches from his very pressing problem. He lifted her foot, stood up, put her foot on the couch, and walked toward the door. And smashed his elbow right into a box.

It crashed. Loudly. Things broke. He swore. Also loudly.

Annie was up next to him in a flash. When he dared look at her, she was staring at the box, her face more wounded than her foot.

He bent, righted the box, and pulled it open. "I'm sorry," he said, meaning it. "I don't know what I was thinking. I'll replace anything broken. I mean it. You just let me know what I can do..."

She was down by him so fast he almost fell back. Grabbing the box from his hands, she held it close to her chest. "Don't worry about it," she said. "There's nothing of value in here. You don't have to pay for anything."

He noticed the death grip she had on the box.

Was that hair he saw poking out of the top? Blond hair?

She stood. "Thanks for looking at the cut, Sheriff. I mean it. But I really have a lot to do tonight."

He stood up, too. He could have felt worse, although he didn't see how. At least his previous emergency was gone. He looked at her again, seeing past that pretty nose to the sad look in her eyes. He'd broken something special. Something she cared about. Well, he'd just have to find out what, and make it right. No matter what she said.

"I'll be leaving," he said, walking to the door. "I'm sorry. I don't know what else to say."

She didn't look at him. "It's all right. Honest. I appreciate you coming over."

He looked at her for a long minute, hoping she'd say something more. After a while, he walked out, feeling lower than the heel he'd just tended.

THE PHONE was ringing as he opened his apartment door. He hurried. It had to be business. No one called him just to chat.

"Sheriff Collins."

"Dan, it's Julie."

"What's the matter? Reese finish up all the ribs by himself?"

"No, Dan. It's serious."

He straightened. Reese's wife wasn't one to get hysterical. If she said it was serious, she meant it. "What's wrong?"

"It's my Barbie."

He moved the receiver away from his ear and stared at it. It was his phone. He put it back to his ear. "What?"

"My Barbie. It's missing."

"Uh..."

"Oh, for heaven's sake. It's a collector's Barbie."

"Uh..."

He could hear the frustration in her sigh. "Dan, it's worth almost three thousand dollars."

"It's what?"

"You heard me."

"A Barbie doll? Like from when you were a kid?"

"Yes! This one is very valuable. And it's missing."

He tried to wrap his mind around the idea of a doll being worth three thousand dollars, but gave it up after a minute. "Where was it the last time you saw it?"

"Where it always is. In the basement. On the shelf."

"You don't think one of the kids at the party just borrowed it to play with it?"

"They couldn't. It's behind the glass door. Locked. Besides, Reese and I have been on the phone for two hours. We've spoken to everyone. No one has seen it."

"Okay. Why don't you come on down to the station tomorrow morning? Let me get some more information about this Barbie. We'll get her back for you."

"I know you will," she said, her voice catching a little. "Dan?"

"Yeah?"

"I don't like to mention it. It's probably got nothing to do with my Barbie at all, but..."

"Go on."

"There was only one person we don't know at the barbecue."

4

ANNIE BLINKED at the light hitting her eyes. She hadn't realized the sun would be quite so bright in the morning. Her apartment in Houston was always a little too dark. It was kind of cheerful this way; maybe she wouldn't get blinds.

As she swung out of bed, she felt a tug in her arm muscles. All that moving, and she still wasn't finished. That was what today was for. Making this place a home, albeit a temporary one. She wanted to go to the market, find the post office, and she wanted to stop by the YMCA to meet her new boss. It was going to be a good day.

She hurried then, rushing through her shower and quickly getting dressed. When she finally got to the living room, she was fairly humming with energy, but she stopped as she looked at her couch. It wasn't a very attractive thing. Brown, with lumpy cushions. But that wasn't what made her pause. She remembered the sheriff sitting there. Dan Collins. The man she was sent here to meet.

He wasn't what she expected. Although how she could have expected much after just reading a paragraph in a singles' magazine wasn't clear to her, but she realized she'd had some preconceived ideas. One, that his looks wouldn't affect her. Normally looks didn't. But there was something about Dan's face that she liked. A lot. No, it was probably his height. She tried to remember if she'd ever been out with anyone over six feet tall, and decided she hadn't. Dan must be at least six-three. With that big chest and narrow waist, he was something of a hunk. Now, that was something she didn't say often about her academic colleagues.

She also liked the fact that she'd flustered him. Both at the picnic and here in the apartment. He might look strong enough to stop bullets with his hands, but she had the feeling he was a pussycat underneath all that brawn.

Not that it mattered. She only had to meet him officially once more, then her obligation to Rachel would be satisfied. Matter of fact, it might be wise to get that meeting over with quickly. Forget about Dan and dive into her summer project.

But first, breakfast.

She slipped on her tennis shoes, ran a brush through her hair, grabbed her purse and set out to explore Harlen.

"SHE'S A COLOR MAGIC, in a cardboard box, midnight-black."

"The doll is midnight black?"

"No, her hair."

"I see." Dan filled out the description of the

missing Barbie, finding it hard to believe that his sister-in-law even had a doll, let alone was so upset at losing it. "Now, how much did you say it was worth?"

"Thirty-one-hundred. Probably more now."

"Are you insured?"

"Yes, but that's not the point. This is an M.I.P. An N.R.F.B!"

"A what?"

Julie, normally unflappable Julie, looked at him with quivering lips. "Mint in Package. Never Removed from the Box."

"And that's important?"

She sighed. "Yes, Dan. That's important. It's what sets the value. If the person who stole her takes her out, plays with her, messes her up, she'll just be another doll." Julie reached over with a manicured hand and grasped his arm. "You can't let that happen, Dan."

"So you don't have any idea who might have taken the doll? You sure it wasn't one of the kids at the party?"

She shook her head and Dan noticed that the part in her hair was slightly crooked. That convinced him more than anything else that this was serious. Julie was meticulous, and the only other times he'd seen her with even one hair out of place was when she'd been in labor.

"No little girl who might just think the Barbie was pretty?"

"No little girl could have opened the glass cabinet. It was jimmied. Is that right? Opened without a key?"

He nodded. "Yes, that's the right term, but it's not such an easy thing to do. Are you sure someone didn't swipe your key?"

"Yes." She opened her purse and brought out a very large key ring. "See?"

"But during the party—"

"Dan, my purse was in my bedroom. In the closet. Underneath my coat. No one even went in there."

He wasn't so sure, but he wasn't going to argue with her about it. "Okay."

"The thing is, you have to get her back for me soon," Julie said. "There's a very important conference coming up, and if I don't have her back by then, why..." She reached inside her purse once more and brought out a crocheted tissue holder. Using only her index finger and thumb, she lifted a tissue and raised it delicately to the corner of her right eye. "It won't be the end of the world," she said softly. "But it will break my heart."

Dan sighed. There was no way he could let this go. Not that he would have, even if it wasn't his sister-in-law who'd asked him for help. A theft had occurred, and it was his responsibility to find the stolen property. What he didn't know was how. If someone had taken her car, or her jewelry, the procedures would be clear. But a Barbie doll? He doubted that his usual suspects were involved, even peripherally.

"Do you think she's involved?"

"Who?" Dan asked.

"That new girl. Annie. The one who your sister seems so high on."

"I don't know. She doesn't seem the type."

"But maybe that's just what she wants us to think. That she wouldn't be the type. Why, what do we really know about her? Dan, I think you need to stick close to her. Find out about her past. Her reasons for being here. I mean why would a professor from a big university like Baylor want to come to a dinky little town like Harlen just to work for the Y? It sounds fishy to me."

"I'll check her out," he said, looking over his robbery report to make sure he'd gotten all the details. "Among other things."

"My instincts tell me she's the one," Julie said vehemently. "So don't you let her out of your sight more than you have to. I mean it, Dan. All the evidence points in one direction."

"I'll take your advice under consideration," he said as he stood up. "I'm sure you have a busy schedule for the day, so I won't keep you any longer."

Julie frowned at him, but she didn't squabble. She just got up, ran a hand over her hair, closed her purse, and walked out the door.

Dan made his way over to the coffeepot. Mike Thomas leaned against the file cabinet, drinking from his Dallas Cowboys mug. "What's up?"

Dan shook his head. "Did you know that Barbie dolls can be worth three thousand dollars?"

"More than that, even," Mike said.

Dan looked at his deputy. "You know about Barbie dolls?"

The younger man nodded. "I saw it on television. An infomercial. They're a big collector item. Lots of women buy 'em and trade 'em. Keep 'em for their kids."

"Julie has one. It was stolen."

Mike chewed on that for a while as he sipped his coffee. "Could be a kid. Didn't get a doll for Christmas."

Dan finished putting sugar in his cup and gave it a stir. "It was in a locked cabinet."

"Kids are pretty clever these days."

Dan smiled. Mike was only twenty-two, barely more than a kid himself. "You seem pretty familiar with this whole thing," he said. "Why don't you look into it?"

Mike shook his head. "She's your sister-in-law."

"I know. But it doesn't matter who finds the doll, as long as it gets found."

"Don't think so," Mike said.

Dan took a long drink of the lukewarm coffee, pondering his next step.

"Might be that new gal," Mike said, after a while.

"Might. But I doubt it."

"Won't be too hard to figure it out. Living next door and all."

"Yeah. Guess so."

Mike put his mug on the counter and walked away, heading for the door. Dan watched him, and thought about his neighbor. What *was* a professor doing in Harlen? He'd asked her at the barbecue, but she hadn't answered. And he hadn't forgotten about the blond hair he'd glimpsed in the box in her apartment. Maybe checking her out wasn't such a bad idea. Like Julie said. Stick close to her for a bit. Get to know her. Do a little digging. It was his job, after all. Nothing personal.

THE TOWN WAS all she'd hoped it would be. Small, a little old-fashioned, singular. From what she'd been able to deduce on her travels so far, the main meeting place was the Green Shade Diner, where, it seemed, everyone came at least once a day for a meal and a dose of gossip. The news evidently traveled fast, because everyone in the diner knew who she was, what she was doing here, and that she lived next door to Dan Collins.

That seemed to be the most exciting tidbit. She'd been in the booth twenty minutes, and already she'd learned that Dan had been married to an "awful young thing," who'd taken him to the cleaners, that he used to be a rodeo champ, that his daddy had been sheriff, and his daddy before that, and that Dan preferred the peach pie, but he'd settle for apple.

The information had come from the waitress, the mailman and a woman named Sylvia, all of whom had sat down across from her without so much as a how-do-you-do. They didn't hesitate to ask her questions, either. Was she married? Did she like her apartment? Had she tried the peach pie?

Finally, her guests had left, giving her a moment to reflect on her day, and to appreciate the excellent club sandwich. Oh, all the folks at the other tables watched her keenly, but no one joined her in the booth.

All the attention probably should have bothered her, but it didn't. She tried to imagine something similar happening in Houston, but of course, that wasn't likely. Houston, for all its museums, theaters and shopping could never be called a cozy town, and that's what she was looking for. Cozy. It did occur to her that cozy and nosy seemed to be more or less interchangeable, but that was okay. She'd like to learn about her neighbors. And one in particular. So wasn't it convenient that everyone felt compelled to tell her about him?

It was clear he was very well-thought-of. And that his ex-wife wasn't. She had been a stranger, too. She'd come to Harlen when she was in high school, which made her suspect from the beginning. Annie hadn't pointed out that by that logic, she was suspect herself.

So why was everyone being so nice to her? So

forthright? She'd imagined having to earn their trust, to build acquaintances that would slowly lead to friendships. But then, she'd never lived in a small town, and had no idea how one worked.

She'd have a lot to put in her letter to Rachel. Thinking of her sister made her a little uneasy. She hoped that Rachel was doing okay, and not getting into trouble.

This was the kind of place she and Rachel should have grown up in. Not a big city. What was that African saying? It takes a village to raise a child? Annie would have been grateful for an aunt, let alone a whole village. But she'd done the best she could, and although Rachel had a real knack for trouble, she was a good person at heart.

It would be nice, however, to really enjoy her stay in this little town without worry. Not a chance. Worrying about Rachel had become a part of her, like breathing. She supposed it would be that way until they were both old and gray.

"You ready for that slice of pie?"

Annie looked up to see Karen, her waitress, standing next to the booth. "I'd like that, thanks."

Karen put an enormous slice of peach pie in front of her, then filled her coffee cup. "You tell me if that isn't the best dang pie you've ever had in your whole life. My mama won three gold medals with that pie. State medals, not some local nonsense."

Annie saw that Karen wasn't going to leave until she tried it, so she obliged. Her mouth fairly danced with the taste of it. This *was* the best dang pie she'd ever had. "It's fabulous! Ambrosial!"

Karen gave her a slow smile, then nodded, as if she'd made a quick decision on the spot. "You wait right there."

Annie couldn't imagine what that was about. Karen hurried off toward the kitchen without another word. In her absence, Annie took another bite of pie and knew she'd have to watch it this summer. Once a week. Maybe twice. No, once. Or maybe she'd work out a little harder and go ahead with twice. After dinner. Sunday dinner.

Karen appeared once more. She put down another slice of pie right across from Annie.

"I couldn't," Annie said. "Not so soon. I'm not even finished with this piece."

"That isn't for you, honey."

"Then who's it for?"

Karen turned to face the door. "Him."

A second went by, then the door opened, making the little bell above it jingle. Dan Collins walked in, and Annie couldn't help but notice that his shoulders practically filled the doorway, and that he looked rugged and handsome in his uniform. Of course, she preferred him in jeans, mostly because the jeans hugged him closer. She'd wager a month's pay that he had a six-pack stomach. Rippled and buff and tight as a drum. With just the right amount of hair on his chest. Dark and soft and curly.

She swallowed hard as he approached.

"Afternoon, Karen," he said as he looked around the room, presumably for his slice of pie.

"Dan," she said, nodding.

"Where is it?"

"Right here," Karen said, moving aside so he could see in Annie's booth. "Thought you might like to sit awhile with your neighbor. Make her welcome."

Annie saw the color rise on his cheeks. She had to hold back a grin when she saw the man take off his hat, look down and actually shuffle his feet in embarrassment. There was something utterly charming about a man of his size being disarmed like that. Especially when she was the reason.

"You don't have to," she said. "If you'd rather be alone, I understand."

"No, it's not... Okay. Well." Dan started to move to another table, then stopped. He looked at her, then Karen. His blush deepened, and Annie stole a glance at the waitress. She was giving him a warning look, as if he was going to get a whipping if he didn't sit down. What an odd town this was.

Dan walked back to her booth and slid into his seat. "Do you mind?" he asked.

"Not at all. I'm grateful for the company."

"That's better," Karen said. "I'll be back with your milk."

Annie studied the sheriff. He seemed engrossed in the peach pie, although he didn't make a move to eat it. She realized she didn't know many shy people. Almost no shy men. She rather liked it in him. He went with the town, with its hand-painted signs and its horse hitch by the post office. She looked at his hands. Working man's hands. Big, strong, callused. He made her think of Gary Cooper.

"How you getting along?" he asked.

She looked up only to find his gaze on her. He must have been doing the same thing she had— sizing up the person sitting opposite him. She wondered if his conclusions had been as generous as her own. "Fine, thanks. I've spent the day exploring. Nice town you have here."

"We like it."

"I stopped by the Y. It's a lot bigger than I expected."

"That's where you're going to work, right?"

She nodded. "Starting on Tuesday."

"Art, is it?"

"That's right."

"I thought you were a sociology teacher."

"Professor, actually. But I've always loved drawing and painting. I even do a little sculpting from time to time. And I love working with kids."

"Uh-huh."

He kept staring at her, not touching his pie, hardly moving at all. She reached for her coffee, more to have something to do than because she was thirsty.

"How'd you find out about the job?"

She coughed, quickly putting down her cup. "Pardon?"

"How'd you find out about the job? We didn't advertise in Houston."

"Is this your way of making me feel welcome?"

He looked away for a moment, then back, his dark brown gaze unapologetic. "I'm just curious," he said. "It's a small town. Most people leave small towns like this. They don't often come back."

"My sister found out about the job, actually. I'm not sure how. She knows how much I've always wanted to come to a place like this, especially if I could work with kids."

"A place like this?"

"A small town. A place where you know your neighbors. Where it's not necessary to lock your doors at night."

"Well, we do know our neighbors, but I wouldn't advise not locking your doors. We have crime here. Not like the big cities, but enough." His brows creased, as his gaze locked onto hers. "We've just had a robbery, as a matter of fact."

"Oh?"

"At the barbecue. Yesterday."

"The one I went to?"

He nodded, never moving his eyes from her.

"That's awful."

"Yeah, it is. A doll was stolen. A very expensive doll."

"Really? A doll?"

"A Barbie doll."

She grinned. "Honestly?"

"Worth about three thousand dollars."

"Yes, I understand they can be worth that much and more."

"So you know about collector Barbies, eh?"

She sat back, wondering what this was all about. "Just from what I've seen on TV."

He nodded slowly. "You don't collect them then?"

"No, I don't. I haven't had a Barbie for years."

He didn't say anything more. He just kept watching her. Even when Karen came back to the table and put down a large glass of milk.

"He making you feel welcome?" she asked.

"Very," Annie said. "If you ignore the fact that he thinks I'm a thief."

5

DAN TOYED with the idea of just getting up and walking out of the diner, but then Karen would spread the news and he'd basically have to leave town for good. Which actually wasn't such a bad idea. Not after how he'd handled this.

He'd acted like a rookie, blundering in feetfirst, totally abandoning his carefully thought-out plan, making a first-class ass of himself, and why? Because when he looked at Annie Jones, he couldn't seem to think straight.

He'd wanted to be subtle. He'd wanted to lay the groundwork for further investigation without arousing her suspicion. He'd wanted to gain her trust.

To say he'd blown it was an understatement.

"What are you talking about?" Karen said, her accusing gaze landing squarely on him. "What's she talking about, Dan?"

He looked at Annie, at the hint of anger behind her smile, at her eyes daring him to explain himself. "I may have given you the wrong impression," he said, hating the way he sounded. "I wasn't implying…"

"But you were." Annie put her napkin on the

table and turned to Karen. "May I have the check, please?"

"He's got it," Karen said.

"Oh, no," Annie said. "I'll pay for my own lunch, thank you."

Dan leaned forward and caught her hand before she had a chance to reach for her purse. "No, please. Let me. It's the least I can do after— I didn't mean to make you uncomfortable."

Annie's gaze moved slowly to their hands, and he looked down, too. God, she was so small. His fingers wrapped around her wrist with plenty of room to spare. He felt as though he was holding on to a bird, so delicate and vulnerable that the slightest move would break her. There, under his thumb, he felt her pulse. A steady, rapid beating that he recognized somehow, as if it was an echo of his own heart, and not a separate rhythm at all.

"Fine," Annie said, her voice a little high and breathless. "Pay if you'd like, but I have to go."

"Wait," Dan said as he removed his hand slowly.

"Why?" Her gaze came up to meet his, and the anger he'd seen a few seconds ago had disappeared, replaced by curiosity.

He cast about for something to say, some reason that wouldn't make him look like a bigger fool. He couldn't tell her the truth. Neither truth. That he suspected her of being a Barbie thief, or that he found himself inexplicably drawn to her.

"There's a fund-raiser tonight at the Y. For my brother, Reese."

"You want me to donate money?"

Dan frowned. "No. I want you to come with me."

"Why?"

He felt his temperature rise and his face turn red. He wondered again how she managed to fluster him so thoroughly. Maybe if he didn't look at her. He switched his gaze to his hands. "I thought I might introduce you around. Most everyone will be there. Kirstie, and Frank... And, well, we're neighbors and all."

"I see."

He dared another glance at her. It wasn't a smart move. Damn, she was a pretty thing. That blond hair of hers shimmered in the café light, moving ever so slightly as she breathed. Her eyes were big and beautiful, but intelligent, too, as if they could see right through him into his thoughts. "So, you'll come?" he asked, his voice so gruff and low he had to clear his throat.

She nodded, making her hair dance again. "I'd like that. Thank you."

He stood up quickly, shaking the table and his untouched coffee. "Seven o'clock. Your place?"

"Okay."

He dug into his pocket and pulled out a twenty and tossed it on the table. Without another word, he turned and left the diner, knowing full well if he stayed another moment he'd just stick his foot in his mouth again. It didn't help to hear Karen's laughter follow him out the door.

ANNIE LOOKED at the pile of clothes on her bed, then at the mirror. She debated changing yet again, back to the first dress she'd tried on, but decided this one would do. It wasn't anything special, just a blue sundress, but it was on the short side. On the other hand, the material felt good and it flattered her figure, so that was that.

She started to hang up the discards, and wondered why she cared so much what she looked like. Oh, sure, she was going to meet new people, but it wasn't people in general she was thinking about. It was Dan. She had to admit it—she wanted to make a good impression on him.

It wasn't just his shyness that appealed to her. It was also the way he looked at her, as if he could see right inside her. It was his gruff voice, and his incredibly soft touch. She liked his face, playing the details over and over in her mind, especially his smile with those straight white teeth and the small dimple on his right cheek. Wouldn't Rachel just go out of her mind if she knew Annie was so intrigued?

Maybe it was because everything was new and strange, or maybe it was because she hadn't been out with anyone except a professor for so long, but Annie felt an anticipation that made her pulse speed up and her throat tighten. It wasn't a Christmas-morning kind of anticipation, more like the beginning of school when all the possibilities lay before her in a series of days and weeks. She had a whole summer to find out about Dan. About living in a small town. About what she wanted to do with herself.

Just that was heady enough. Thinking about her future and her plans, instead of worrying about Rachel to the exclusion of everything else. Annie tried to remember the last time she'd put herself first. It had to be back when she was in college, selecting her major. Even then, she hadn't chosen art, but something more practical so she could be sure of getting a job.

But not this summer. This was her summer, wrapped up in a big pink bow. She didn't honestly think anything was going to come of Rachel's matchmaking scheme. The odds against that were, what, a million to one? On the other hand, there was nothing wrong with trying him on for size, was there? He sure was good-looking. Good-looking and big.

She went back to the bathroom and checked her makeup and hair. She brushed her teeth again, then sprayed a little lilac perfume on her pulse points. Then she looked at the clock and saw she was an hour and forty minutes early.

HE HELD HER arm as they walked into the YMCA. The whole place was decorated in red, white and blue streamers, balloons, and posters calling for Reese Collins's reelection. Music blared from large speakers and tables filled with food, drink, buttons, hats and pamphlets lined the walls. Folks mingled shoulder to shoulder, with some dancing going on in the center. It was a big party for a town this size, and Annie wondered why they needed the party at all. It seemed to her everyone who could vote was here, all supporting Reese. But maybe her perception of the size of Harlen was off.

Dan led her through the crowd, and Annie was a little taken aback at how the people stared at her. She wished she'd been here a week or two already, so her presence wasn't such a sight. The good thing was that most of the new faces smiled at her.

Dan came to a stop and leaned down, never releasing his light hold on her arm. "Would you like some punch?"

She nodded. When he left her, she rubbed the skin where his hand had been, feeling the traces of heat he'd left behind. She watched him make his way to the side table, so graceful for a guy his size. From this angle, she could see that he was really quite slender in the hips, but his chest was so broad and his legs were so long, he gave the impression that he was larger than life. Especially in those jeans. And that western-cut shirt.

"He used to ride bulls, you know."

Annie jumped at the voice in her ear. An older man, someone she'd never seen before, stood very close to her. Close enough for her to know that he must be spiking his punch with some pretty strong stuff. "Pardon?" she asked, having to shout a little over the noise.

"Dan Collins. Rode the rodeo all through high school. Even after. Got him some trophies, and a broken collarbone."

"Really?"

"Yep. Could have been an athlete, that one. Football. But he wanted to be like his daddy."

"I'm Annie Jones," she said, holding out her hand. "I don't think we've met."

The man, who she guessed was in his sixties, took her hand and pumped it a couple of times, then let it go. He smiled a big toothy grin, which made his eyes crinkle up to almost nothing. "Hugh Stemple. Lived in Harlen all my life. Watched that boy grow up."

"Are you related to him?"

"Nope. Just a neighbor. Lived next door to his daddy's place for forty-six years."

"Wow."

"Yep."

Annie tried to think of a follow-up question, but Hugh didn't give her a chance. He sipped his punch and walked away, as if he'd finished his oral report and wanted to leave before the grade.

While she tried to figure it out, a woman touched her arm. She was in her thirties, blond, with really big hair and a considerable amount of makeup. "You're the new girl."

Annie nodded.

"Annie Jones, right?"

She nodded again.

"Sylvia Trainer. I work part-time at the bookstore."

"Nice to meet you."

"Dan's a reader. He doesn't flaunt it, but he's a reader, all right."

"I see," Annie said, even though she didn't. Why would someone she didn't know tell her about Dan's reading habits?

"He likes biographies, mostly. But some of that Tom Clancy, too."

"Yes, well, Clancy is good."

"He's six-foot-five, you know."

"Tom Clancy?"

Sylvia laughed. "No, Dan. I don't know how tall Clancy is."

"Have you lived here all your life, too?"

"Me? Lord, yes. Went to school with Reese. But that Dan, he was always something."

"I'll bet."

"You're not like the other one."

"The other one?"

"Melissa."

The way Sylvia said the name, she could have been talking about a poisonous snake. Annie was just about to ask who this Melissa was when Dan came back, armed with two glasses of punch. He handed one to Annie, then gave a tight smile to his neighbor.

"How you doing, Sylvia?" Dan asked.

"I'm fine. I was just telling Annie here about the bookstore."

"I'm sure she'll be by before too long."

Sylvia winked at Annie. "Not if she has something better to do."

Annie smiled, although the comment seemed odd. Sexual, actually. But no, that couldn't be right.

Sylvia winked once more, this time at Dan, then she left.

"Sorry that took so long," he said. "You hungry?"

Annie shook her head. "No, not really." She let her gaze wander briefly over the crowd. "Big turnout."

"Most everyone in town."

"So who's he running against?"

"Carl Porter. Same as ever. But Reese will win. He always does."

"So why the fund-raiser?"

Dan shrugged. "It's actually more like an excuse for a party. The money they collect pays for the food and the music."

"Really?"

"If it's not an election year, we call it a summer dance."

Annie grinned. "I like it."

"Yeah, we do, too."

"So far, Harlen is pretty much what I'd pictured."

"Yeah?"

"Nice folks. Close-knit."

"Nosy."

"Well, that, too. But it's a good kind of nosy. They care."

"They're mostly just bored."

"I don't believe you."

"Stay here for a few years. You'll see."

Annie didn't say anything. She just let the thought linger for a moment, like tasting wine on her palate.

"Hey, Dan."

Annie turned to the singsong voices behind them. Two women, twins, in their early twenties, stood side by side, looking up at the sheriff.

"Evening Lucy, Linda."

"We heard you had a new friend." The women giggled in tandem.

"She's just here for the summer. Annie Jones, these are the Finch twins."

Annie nodded, not missing the way the ladies played with their respective hairdos, swished their hips back and forth, and generally displayed all the subtlety of a biology-textbook lesson on flirting.

"Well, maybe she'll be able to talk you into having some fun," Lucy said. At least Annie thought it was Lucy.

"Yeah. You've become such an old stick-in-the-mud." Linda moved to one side of Annie, and Lucy moved to the other. As if on cue, they both leaned in and whispered, "Good luck, honey."

Then they walked toward the dance floor, moving in unison.

"Wow," she said.

"Don't pay any attention to them," Dan said, shaking his head. "They've got more time on their hands than good sense."

"They seemed to like you."

"They know better."

"Pardon?"

"They're just trying to rile me up." He looked down at her, and his eyes grew serious. "Everyone in Harlen knows I'm not looking for that kind of thing."

"What kind of thing would that be?"

"You'll hear it sooner or later, so I'll just tell you. I was married. It was a mistake. One I won't be making again."

Annie felt her chest constrict. She almost asked him straight out why he put the ad in the magazine if he didn't want to marry again, but then she remembered Kirstie's warning. Maybe it wasn't a general pronouncement. Maybe it was his not-so-subtle way of saying he wasn't interested in her in particular. Whatever the case, his position was clear. She felt her face heat up, and she looked away.

It wasn't as if she'd told him she was interested. Not in so many words. He had no way of knowing she'd been thinking of him all afternoon. So why was she so embarrassed? It was nothing. She'd only known him a couple of days, for heaven's sake. But it didn't matter. She couldn't stand here, not anymore. She'd blundered, badly, and it shook her up. She straightened her shoulders and met his gaze. "Would you excuse me, please? It's a little loud in here, and I've gotten myself a headache."

His brows came together in concern and he touched her arm again. The same heat was there, but this time, she felt burned. She moved until his hand dropped. "Would you like me to take you home?"

"No, thanks. I'll walk. It's not far."

"Hey, no. It's too crazy here for me, too. I'll just get the truck."

"No. Please. I'd rather walk." She found a trash can and tossed her paper cup. "Thanks for bringing me," she said.

"Wait."

She didn't. She walked to the door quickly, maneuvering between the citizens of Harlen. Their smiles didn't look so friendly anymore. No one seemed the least surprised that she was leaving alone. They all knew he wasn't looking for "that kind of thing." Wasn't that what he'd said? So she was just a stranger, in a strange town, who'd been played for a fool. No big deal. It was only a summer. Three months. It wasn't as if she'd lost anything, right? Just a silly little fantasy. A tiny drop of hope.

The air outside was warm and moist, and the whole town in front of her seemed dark and quiet. She walked slowly down Main, not seeing a single living soul. It took a long time for the noise from the party to fade, but finally it did. And with it, her dream of a summer romance.

6

THE SECOND BARBIE was reported missing shortly after midnight. Jessie Higgins called Dan on his home phone, her voice shaky and her tone apologetic.

"Don't worry, Jessie," Dan said. "I wasn't sleeping, and I don't mind. Just tell me where you last saw the doll."

"She was in my car. Dan, I didn't lock the door. I can't believe it. I should have locked it. But I didn't."

"It's okay," he said, rubbing his dog's belly as they shared the couch. "Take it easy, and lay it all out for me."

"I was taking her to Margaret's. We're going to the convention, you know. Together. And Margaret was going to pack mine with hers, you see. So they would be safe."

"Margaret has dolls, too?"

"Three. Very expensive. Much more than mine."

"What's yours worth?"

"Only about fifteen hundred dollars. She's a Hair Happening redhead. New in the box. Never opened. From 1974. Actually, I bought her in

1977, but she was made in '74. I was going to give her to my niece, but now..."

"Your niece will have her, Jessie."

"Who could do such a thing, Dan?"

He heard the older woman sniffle, and he grimaced. Jessie Higgins never cried. She wasn't the type. She was a tough woman who'd gone through two son-of-a-bitch husbands and never complained. Even when she caught Albert with the dog groomer.

"I'm gonna find out, Jess. Now, where were you parked?"

"On Main. A block from your apartment, as a matter of fact. You had to pass my car to get home."

"And the doll was in the front seat?"

"Squarely in the center. Oh, I'm such an old fool. The streetlight came right in the windshield. Anyone walking past would have seen her. But no one I know would do such a thing. Everyone knows my car. It would have to have been a stranger, but we don't have any strangers in town, do we?"

Dan's hand stilled. There was only one stranger, and it was his next-door neighbor. Since she'd been in Harlen, two valuable dolls had disappeared. The logical conclusion was that Annie Jones was involved. But he didn't believe it. Something didn't ring true. He had a sense about her, a feeling. Not that his feelings were always reliable. Hell, he'd had a feeling he was going to be with Melissa for the rest of his life. "Jessie, I don't want you to worry about this. Just go on to bed, and first thing in the morning, I'll get on this. I'll get your doll back."

"The convention's in two weeks, Dan."

"I heard something about that."

"It's my first vacation in five years. I've got a hotel reservation. I bought material for my new dress."

Dan sighed. Great. "Okay, Jess. I hear you. Now you go on to sleep, and I'll see you in the morning."

Jessie sniffed. "Thanks, Dan. 'Night."

Dan hung up the phone, and turned to his dog beside him on the couch, who'd managed to roll on his back with all four legs sticking up in the air. "What do you think, Cougar? You think Annie is stealing Barbie dolls?"

The Lab moaned and wiggled his rear end, waiting for the scratching to continue. Dan obliged. His thoughts, however, were not on Cougar, but on the beautiful woman from next door.

He hadn't stayed at the fund-raiser long after she left. What was the point? People kept wanting to talk, mostly about Annie, and he didn't care to discuss the subject. Especially not with his family. Dan might not be a rocket scientist, but he knew when he was being set up. The whole damn town seemed to want to push him into Annie's arms. To get him married again. As if they had all conveniently forgotten the consequences of his last marriage.

What was it about folks that they couldn't stand to see a single man? Dan got along just fine. He had his job, and Cougar, and his apartment. What did he need a woman for?

Well, there was *that*, but for *that* he didn't need a wife. Not even a girlfriend. He just needed to find himself a woman who was looking for the same thing he was. He knew they existed. Women who didn't want the complications of a relationship. Just the fun. Safe fun.

His gaze shifted to the wall that separated his apartment from Annie's. She was here for the summer. Then she was going back to her job and her life in Houston. What if she wanted something...temporary? Something for the summer, and no more? He hadn't considered that. No. If that's all she wanted, she wouldn't have looked so surprised tonight when he'd made his intentions clear. Besides, Annie wasn't the type. She was looking for a husband, all right. That is, if she wasn't just looking for an expensive doll collection.

She would have passed by Jessie's car on her way home. He found it easy to picture Annie in her pale blue dress, her blond hair shining in the light from the street lamp, opening the car door and plucking the boxed doll from the front seat. It was even easier to picture her putting the doll in one of those packing boxes, then going to her bedroom and taking off that pale blue dress to get ready for bed. Her skin would be warm, soft, smooth and then she'd reach behind her back to unclasp her bra and—

Cougar's moan snapped him out of his little trip down voyeurs' lane. But his body took a while to come to its senses. So, okay, he did need a woman. Seriously. Very, very soon. He'd find one, too. Not here, though. Not in Harlen. He'd go over to Twin Forks, where not so many folks knew him. There was that pool bar on Fourteenth. He could meet someone there.

For now, he needed to calm down and get some rest. If Annie was involved with the Barbie thefts, he'd get to the bottom of it. If she wasn't, he'd find out who was. It was all a matter of doing his job the way his daddy'd taught him.

Hell, he'd kill two birds with one stone. He'd go out with Annie so the town matchmakers would leave him be, and he'd investigate the Barbie doll thefts at the same time. As far as police work went, it wasn't such a bad assignment. As long as he remembered who he was and what he was doing.

Dan got up off the couch and went to his bedroom. By the time he'd crawled under the covers, Annie had unclasped her bra, and he watched in his mind's eye as the slip of material fell to the floor.

ANNIE SAID YES, even though she'd meant to say no. But there it was. The word was out there, floating in space, clear as a bell.

"Great," Dan said. "I'll pick you up at seven."

"Well..."

"Nothing fancy," he went on. "Jeans. It's a pretty laid-back place."

"Um..."

"I've got to run. See you tonight."

Then she heard the dial tone. What had she gone and done? Was she nuts? Why was she going out with Dan, when she knew very well that he wasn't interested in romance? Was her subconscious trying to tell her something? Like maybe that romance wasn't what she was interested in, either?

Annie hung up the phone and went back to the dining-room table, where she was going over art books for her class. She sipped her iced tea and studied the big pictures in the first-grade text. But her mind wasn't on red balloons.

It was on sex.

Sex, just for the sake of sex. Hot. Passionate. Illicit. Sweaty. Just like she'd read about. But, of course, had never experienced for herself.

Why was that? How had she gone this long without even once dipping her toe into that forbidden pond? Not that she was a virgin. Oh, no. Ralph Templeton had seen to that. And then there'd been Jerry for most of grad school. Finally, briefly, Peter. But none of those experiences could in any way be described as illicit. Or terribly passionate, come to think of it. If they had been sweaty, it was only as a result of a bad air conditioner.

She'd always known that other women had much better luck with sex than she had, but it hadn't bothered her too much. Maybe that wasn't right. It probably would have bothered her a lot if she'd let herself think about it. But she didn't. Instead, she worried about Rachel.

But Rachel wasn't here. So that just left her. And the depressing realization that she was twenty-seven years old without one sexual regret.

How sad was that? Didn't every woman deserve to have at least one torrid affair that made her blush? One wicked encounter whose memory would go with her to the grave?

Damn it, when was it her turn? Tonight?

She got up quickly and went into the bedroom. Opening her underwear drawer, she sifted through the bras and panties, looking for that silky red bra she'd bought in '95, but it wasn't there. When she looked at what was there, she got even more depressed. White cotton. Functional. Conservative. Boring. Not a teddy, or even a bikini among them, let alone a thong. Although wearing a thong seemed to her the height of discomfort. But how would she know? She'd never tried one on.

She slammed the drawer closed and picked up her purse. She was going to have dinner with Dan tonight, and maybe, if she played her cards right, she could have herself some dessert.

DAN'S HEAD swam with Barbies. And Kens and Skippers, and Brads and Caseys and all the other relatives and friends of Mattel's creation. He'd had no idea. None. There was a Barbie universe out there, where hundreds, no, thousands of women collected, traded, discussed and talked about Barbara Millicent Roberts, a.k.a Barbie. There were newsletters, web sites, books, computer programs, organizations, all dedicated to the doll. And he'd been thrust into the middle of it all. Not that it had helped him much in his investigation. Except to realize that whoever was taking the Barbies was savvy as to the value of the dolls.

While you could go into any toy store and pick up a Barbie for fifteen bucks, there was also a cadre of Barbies that were worth thousands. The collectors were a serious, educated bunch, who understood the value of an unopened box, of a limited edition. They traded as seriously as anyone on Wall Street.

His thief was no dummy. Whoever was going after these dolls wanted some serious cash, and they were going to get it. The beauty of it was, none of the dolls had serial numbers or any kind of individual marking on the box to trace them. Once on the market, they were just out there. Nothing to indicate that they'd ever been stolen.

The major surprise had been how many women in Harlen collected. His sister-in-law, Jessie and Margaret were only the tip of the iceberg. It seemed that the women of Harlen were well-known throughout the Barbie community. Several of them had even been asked to speak on panels at the annual convention. And here he'd thought he knew his town.

He looked into the mirror and wiped the remaining shaving cream off his chin. It was almost time to get Annie. Tonight, he'd find out just how much she knew about Barbie. After a little dinner, a few drinks, he'd bring up the case. He'd listen. He'd learn. By the end of the night he was going to know if his neighbor was a thief or not. He hoped she wasn't.

The truth was, he liked Annie. He liked thinking about her. He'd hate to have to send her to jail. But, he would, if he had to.

SHE KNEW he couldn't see her underwear. It wasn't possible. Her clothes completely covered the lacy black bra and the matching thong panties. Not even a hint was visible. But she felt her cheeks heat anyway. For about the fiftieth time in two hours. He'd glanced down, and that had done it. She'd felt sure he could tell. That her movements, her speech, her posture broadcast the fact that she only looked like a schoolteacher from the outside. But that underneath, she was dressed like a model for Victoria's Secret.

It didn't help that she'd been correct in her assumption that thong panties were, to put it mildly, uncomfortable. She'd spent most of her life adjusting her clothing so that material didn't go where the thong was designed to be. It made it difficult to concentrate on her salad.

"Would you like another beer?" Dan asked.

She shook her head. "I'm fine, thanks."

"You barely ate a thing."

"I had a big lunch," she said.

"They make a hell of a good peach cobbler here. I recommend it."

"Thanks, that sounds great." Annie smiled at him, forcing herself to forget about her underclothes and focus on her objective. She still wanted to explore the idea of having a wild fling with the sheriff, but it was more complicated than she'd imagined. First of all, she wasn't sure if he was interested. She knew he didn't want a romance, but that didn't tell her if he was interested in something, well, briefer. He seemed to like her. He certainly listened attentively. But she was also picking up something else about him. The only way she could describe it was suspicion. He listened a little too well. His questions probed a little too deep.

Maybe he was just naturally inquisitive. He was a sheriff, so that might have something to do with his interest in her past. But that didn't quite explain it. Something was going on with Dan and she couldn't tell if it was sexual, professional, courteous, or just nosy. It made it hard to flirt. And she wasn't good at flirting to begin with.

"So, you were saying about Rachel's blackmail?"

She nodded. "She knew I wouldn't be able to say no. And she sure played her cards right."

"But you said yourself that you'd always wanted to live in a small town."

"That's true. I suppose she was really doing me a favor." Annie stopped for a moment, then decided right there and then to throw caution to the wind. "While I'm here, there are a lot of new things I want to try." She smiled in what she hoped was a seductive manner. "Make new friends," she said, lifting one brow. "Live out some fantasies."

That got his attention. It also made her want to crawl into a hole. Whoa, she'd gone too far. Way over the edge. She was not ready for fantasies, for heaven's sake!

"Care to be more specific?" he asked, his voice lower than she remembered.

"Uh, well, you know. With teaching kids and all."

He gave her a peculiar look, and she busied herself with some lettuce. How was it possible for her to be this inept? First the panty debacle, now this. He must think she was a loon.

"You left the party early last night," he said. "Didn't give yourself a chance to meet many folks."

"I guess I was a little tired."

"But you walked home, didn't you?"

She nodded. "It wasn't far."

"Uh-huh. See anything interesting on your way?"

She heard his casual tone, noted his nonchalant posture, and felt sure that something more was going on. "No, I didn't," she said. "The streets were pretty much empty."

"Too bad," he said, turning his gaze on her. "We had a little robbery. I was hoping you'd seen something."

"Really? Oh, my. What happened?"

"A doll was taken from one of my dispatcher's cars."

"A doll?"

He nodded slowly. "A Barbie doll." He said it with such significance that Annie felt as though he was giving her a secret code.

"Another one?"

Again, he nodded. Slowly. Deliberately. Never taking his eyes off her.

"You certainly do have interesting crimes here. Two Barbies in three days? Wow."

His lips curled slightly. "*Wow* is right. And whoever is stealing them knows they're worth a bundle."

"More than the ones at Wal-Mart, I gather?"

"Considerably."

"Well, then I *am* sorry I didn't see anything."

He didn't say anything at all to that. Just kept

watching her. Played a little with his spoon. Breathed deeply.

"Oh," she said, finally getting it. "You really think I—? Me?" Her cheeks went hot again, but this time it wasn't from embarrassment. How dare he think she would steal someone's doll? He didn't even know her. She remembered the last conversation about a stolen Barbie, how she'd joked that he suspected her, but now it wasn't so funny.

"No, no," he said, reaching over to touch her hand. "I don't think any such thing."

She jerked her hand back. "Why did you ask me out?"

"Huh?"

"Come on. Why? Just last night you said you didn't want anything to do with a woman. So why am I here?"

He looked down but somehow managed to straighten his shoulders at the same time. She could tell he was trying to think, trying to come up with some explanation that wouldn't offend her further. She balled her napkin up and put it on the table. "I did not steal anyone's doll," she said carefully. "Just because a person is new in town, it doesn't make them a thief."

"Now, hold on."

She stood up. "And to think I bought new underwear," she said.

His eyes grew very wide. She slapped her hand to her mouth, appalled that she'd said that aloud.

"You did?" he asked. "For me?"

She didn't know what to do. Where to look. So she did what any normal person would do in her situation. She ran to the bathroom.

7

DAN SIGHED. He'd blown it again. He'd been nervous and that had made him clumsy and now he didn't know what the hell to do.

Annie wasn't the thief. Despite his attempts to be the lousiest sheriff in the state of Texas, he'd figured that out. Her outrage was real, and unless she was a sociopath, her reaction had been genuine. Whoever was stealing Barbies was still at large. Which wasn't his topmost problem at the moment. Annie's flight to hide in the ladies' room took that spot.

The night had been going so well, too. He'd relaxed. He'd enjoyed listening to her stories. She certainly wasn't bad to look at. And damn, that underwear comment changed everything.

Wouldn't it be just like him to ruin things before they got started? Imagine, a gorgeous woman, unattached, living next door for Pete's sake, who was interested in *underwear*, and he'd just made her run for the hills. Slick. Very slick. He ought to write a book.

There had been a time when he'd felt confident around women. Secure. But that was before Melissa had pointed out his flaws. Pointed them out over and over again. He didn't dress the right way, or talk the right way, or know the right people.

On the other hand, Annie wasn't Melissa.

Carefully folding his napkin and putting it down beside his plate, he corralled his gumption to stand up and go get her. Of course he didn't know exactly how, but he had to try.

As he walked toward the bathroom, he saw Logan Baxter sitting with his wife. His deputy smiled at him, but wasn't there a trace of pity in that grin? Had he seen Annie make a run for it? The thought made Dan look at the other diners. There was Gina Painter. Lloyd Braxton. Fanny Porter. The whole Daniels family. All of them staring. All of them smiling sympathetically. By the time he got home tonight, half the town would know he'd blown it with Annie. The other half would hear about it over the watercoolers in the morning.

That was it. He was moving. To a big city. A huge city. New York. Where people knew how to mind their own business.

He'd made it to the ladies' room. Without a plan. Should he just wait? Knock? Go on in? And when he saw her, what was he supposed to say?

This was ridiculous. He felt the gazes of his so-called friends on his back, burning a hole in his shirt. Damn it.

He raised his hand to knock and the door swung out, hitting him square in the face. It wasn't a bad blow, but it did knock him back a step.

"Oh, goodness. Are you all right?"

Annie stood looking up at him, concern creasing her brow.

He rubbed his nose and nodded. "I'm fine."

"Well enough to drive me home?"

He let his hand drop. "What about that cobbler?"

"I don't think so. I have a full schedule tonight. I'm stealing a Barbie at nine, and a Skipper at ten. Then there's the whole Ken thing at midnight."

"Now, Annie..."

"You do not know me well enough to 'Now, Annie' me."

"Do I know you well enough to apologize?"

"You do."

"Then I'm sorry. I didn't mean to imply that you were the thief."

"Of course you did. I was there, remember? I heard your voice."

This wasn't going well. He glanced at the men's-room door and thought about making a break for it, but then he'd be known as a fool *and* a coward. "Granted," he said. "I'll admit I did bring up the whole Barbie thing so I could feel you out about it."

"Why would I want to steal anyone's Barbie? It's absurd."

"They're worth a lot of money."

"Fine. But why me? What did I do that made you even think such a thing?"

"It wasn't personal. You're new in town. No one knows you. I wouldn't have been doing my job without at least checking you out."

"So that *is* why you asked me here."

He dared a glance behind her. Every eye was on them. Every ear waiting to hear the next line. "Don't you people have anything better to do?" he said.

Annie looked then, and he heard her little gasp.

"Welcome to small-town living," he said, taking her arm. "Come on. We're going to continue this in private."

She let him lead her back to the table, where he slapped down several bills. He hung on to her all the way to the front door, where he didn't give the vultures behind him the satisfaction of even one glance back, then they were out in the parking lot. He didn't let her go until they reached his truck, and then just long enough to open the door for her.

"Dan?"

"Yeah?"

"You're not going to like this."

"What now?"

"My purse is inside. Next to the chair."

He wanted to tell her to forget it. He'd buy her a new one. But of course, he couldn't. That's because he was cursed. Born under a bad sign. Destined for humiliation and failure.

"I'll go get it," she said softly.

"No, no. You go on and get in. I'll be right back." The walk to the door was a long one, or at least it felt long. He hesitated a moment to square his shoulders and take a deep breath. Then he pushed on in.

He didn't have to go to the table, though. Because Darlene, the waitress, was standing by the door. Holding out Annie's purse. Grinning.

Without a word, he grabbed the handbag, turned on his heel and left. The laughter followed him halfway back to the truck. He climbed in and handed Annie her purse.

"Sorry," she said.

"No problem." He drove, keeping his eyes on the road. Wishing like hell he'd never met Annie or heard of Barbie or become a sheriff. He'd been right, of course. The smart thing was to forget about women. Live the life of a bachelor. Go to work, come home, pet the dog, go to sleep. It had worked for countless men before him, and it would work for him.

Then he felt something on his sleeve. A feathery touch, light enough for him to mistake it for a breeze, but warm. It was her fingers. He could feel them, each one. As if his shirt wasn't there at all. He swallowed. The sensation in his arm started to spread. Up to his shoulder. Across his chest. Down. Straight down.

"Dan?"

"Yes," he croaked, his voice cracking like a schoolboy's.

"I understand."

He looked down at his very tight jeans, then over to Annie. Then he saw she wasn't referring to his physical condition. Lord, how much could a man humiliate himself before he just plain died?

"I *am* new in town, and you were right to suspect me. Or at least talk to me. If I had been in your shoes, I would have done the same thing."

He breathed. Then again. He needed to speak in a normal voice. He needed to stop acting like a jerk. He didn't know if he could do either.

"But rest assured," she said. "I'm not the Barbie thief. Although I like Barbies. I had several when I was a girl. Played with them constantly. Rachel was a tomboy, but sometimes she'd join me. We didn't have anything as fancy as a Dream House. We used a shoe box. Painted it to look like Barbie's bedroom. I remember my eleventh birthday. My mom had passed away four months before. I didn't think it was going to be much of a birthday. But then my father brought out all these packages. Barbie clothes. My mother had made sure he bought them for me. She knew she wasn't going to be there, but she wanted me to have them. Wasn't that something?"

Dan nodded. He felt himself relax by degrees, although he was still acutely aware of her hand on his arm. He didn't want to speak or move for fear she'd take her hand away. So he just smiled at her and kept on listening.

"I kept them for a long time," she said. "Until college. Then I don't know what happened to them. I think my roommate must have thrown them out or something, because when I left school, they were gone. I hope some little girl found them. They were nice. A prom dress, and a tutu, and a pink suit. With a matching purse and hat. Gosh, I haven't thought about that in years."

"Nice memories," he said.

"Yeah. I guess that's why so many women collect them. Because of the memories."

"I suppose so," he said.

Annie moved, then, taking her hand away. He looked down, somehow expecting to see a mark where she'd touched him, but there was nothing but white shirtsleeve.

"Was there anyone else?" she asked.

"Pardon?"

"Are there any other suspects? Besides me?"

He smiled. "Frankly, no. I don't have any idea who our thief may be."

"Someone who didn't have dolls as a kid?"

"Or someone who understands what a hot Barbie will sell for on the open market."

She laughed. "What an odd world this is. Hot Barbies."

"You're telling me. It's not what I imagined when I went through the academy."

"Maybe there's a Barbie Dream Prison where

people go when they steal the dolls. With striped pajamas and tin cup accessories. Guards sold separately, of course."

"Right. G.I. Joe would be the warden, of course."

She laughed, and he liked the sound a lot. "I love it," she said. "Did you have one?"

"A G.I. Joe?"

"Yeah."

"Nope, can't say that I did. I was pretty much into the rodeo when I was a kid."

"I heard."

"You did?"

"At the fund-raiser. Someone told me you used to be a big deal on the rodeo circuit."

"I wouldn't say big deal. But I won a time or two."

"I can see that's a lie. You probably took every blue ribbon in the state."

He glanced at her, taking a great deal of pleasure in the sparkle in her eyes. Her hand wasn't on his arm anymore, but there was an even better connection between them now. Her humor, her teasing. It had been a long time since a beautiful woman had teased him. He hadn't realized the loss. "What makes you think that?"

"Because you're blushing."

"I'm not. I don't blush."

"Ha. If you were Pinocchio, your nose would have grown two inches."

"I beg your pardon. I don't lie, and I don't blush."

"Like fun."

"You doubting the word of the law, young lady?"

"I am."

"Barbie prison for you. Thirty days."

"Hmm. Well, I know some things about G.I. Joe. I bet I can get out of there for good behavior."

"Oh?"

"Yeah. He may have a chest like a rock, but in other areas, he's um, shall we say...deficient?"

"Hey. It's not his fault. He was still a stud."

"Maybe. But I'm still mad at him." She laughed again. "Embarrassingly enough, when I was little, I didn't realize he wasn't anatomically correct. Imagine my surprise when Tom Lykins from down the block offered to 'show me his.' I was traumatized."

"But Barbie wasn't anatomically correct, either."

"Ah, you're going for logic."

"What can I say? It's a habit I got into, and I just can't shake it."

"Then I imagine this world is a pretty bewildering place for you."

"You have no idea." He looked at her again, and he laughed for the first time in a long, long time.

"Aren't you going to turn?"

He'd almost missed their street. He reached his

hand out to protect Annie when he hit the brakes. Her body lurched forward, despite her seat belt, and he felt a soft mound of flesh underneath his palm. She moved back slowly.

"I, on the other hand, am anatomically correct," she said.

This time, he didn't even try to deny his blush.

"YOU LIKE HIM!"

Annie wanted to deny it. She didn't want Rachel getting any ideas. Nothing had happened, really. Just one nice conversation. They hadn't made any future plans. They hadn't kissed. As far as she knew, he was just a friendly neighbor, nothing more. And yet...

"I can hear you smiling. Did you do it?"

"Rachel! Nothing happened. We had dinner. He accused me of being a thief. We talked about Barbies. Period."

"Wow, that sounds like some dinner. Now explain."

"It's complicated. Someone's stealing collector Barbie dolls, and he thought it might be me."

"Did you explain to him that you're constitutionally incapable of stealing? Or lying? Or even hanging up on phone salespeople?"

"I am not."

"Ha! So when are you going to see him again?"

"I don't know. We didn't make any plans."

"So, invite him over for dinner. Make lasagna. Men love lasagna."

"I'm not going to invite him for dinner. If he wants to see me again, he knows where I am."

"Wake up and smell the '90s woman. Jeez."

"Rachel, he flat out told me he wasn't interested in a relationship."

"Already? Well, there you have it. He's completely thinking about it. You're halfway home."

"Are you joking?"

"No. Why would he even bring it up, if he wasn't thinking about it? I swear, I don't know how you can be so smart and be so dumb."

"Stop, you're making me blush."

"Will you please invite him to dinner? For me?"

"Haven't I done enough for you already?"

"Okay. Then do it for you. Come on, Annie. Admit it. You like this guy. You said yourself he was gorgeous. And funny. And smart."

"I said I thought he was those things. Not that I knew."

"So find out for sure."

"Maybe."

"Maybe my ass. Do it. Don't think. You're always thinking too much. Just pick up the phone and invite him over. And Annie?"

"Yes?"

"Get some new underwear."

"Ha!"

"What?"

"I already did."

Annie yanked the phone away from her ear,

but Rachel's yell made her smile. Of course, she'd been doing that a lot since she'd met Dan Collins.

DAN COLLINS LOST his smile the moment he opened the paper. There, on the front page, was a story about the missing Barbies. A feature article, written by none other than his sister Kirstie, highlighting the fact that "police had no clue" as to who might be stealing the valuable dolls. She might as well have mentioned his name. Everyone in three counties would know exactly who she meant.

He picked up the phone and dialed Kirstie's number at the paper.

"Collins."

"Traitor."

"Oh, dear."

"You got that right. How could you do this to me? You're supposed to be on my side, remember?"

Kirstie didn't respond for a long time. Long enough for him to get really worried. "Kirstie?"

"You're not going to like it."

"I already don't like it."

"You're not going to like it a whole lot."

He sighed. It had promised to be such a good day. The sun was shining, he'd slept like a baby. Dreamed of underwear. "Go on."

"They picked up the story."

"Who?"

"Well. Everyone."

"What do you mean?"

"The wires. They picked up the story. It's gone national."

"What? So now the entire country knows I'm inept?"

"It's not that. I mean, no one thinks that. I didn't even use your name."

"That makes me feel so much better."

"Dan, I didn't realize. I never imagined."

"You didn't think."

"Come on. I said I was sorry."

"Yeah. I'll bet."

Another pause. He closed his eyes, knowing the worst was yet to come.

"Dan?"

"Just say it."

"Um, they're probably gonna show up around noon."

"They?"

"Reporters."

"Oh?"

"And a television crew."

"I see."

"I tried to tell them not to come."

"But they didn't listen."

"Yeah."

"Great. Thanks, Kirstie. I'll remember this, come Christmas. I hope you like coal."

"And Dan?"

"Oh, please. I can't take any more."

"Sorry. But another one's gone."

"Oh, crap. Who's is it?"

"Sylvia Trainer's. She's on her way to see you now."

"Perfect. Just perfect. Well, at least it can't get any worse. Right, Kirstie? Right?"

8

"MY TWIST'N TURN is not going in the same cell as that Wacky Warehouse doll."

"Well, honey, my Snow Princess wouldn't be caught dead with your Twist'n Turn."

"It don't matter as long as they all stay in the box."

"Who's gonna watch 'em? How do we know the thief isn't someone from the sheriff's department. Remember Roswell? Kennedy? It could all be a conspiracy."

"How come Gina ain't here? She's got that Pink Jubilee, don't she? Maybe she's the one. She always did have her eye on my Snow Princess."

Dan surveyed the throng of Barbie-toting women in front of him and debated an immediate career change. "Ladies!"

Everyone stilled and turned to stare at him.

"I assure you, nothing will happen to the dolls. They'll be locked in a cell. I'll have the only key."

"No offense, Dan, but the only way you're going to get my Barbie is to pry her out of my cold, dead fingers."

"Now, Phyllis," he said, astonished at the sixty-something wife of the Episcopalian minister. "I'm not trying to take your doll for keeps. Just until we find out who's stealing them."

"No," she said, her curly white hair trembling with her defiance. "I brought her here for protection, but now that I see this unruly mob, I won't trust her anywhere but in my own home." She turned to face Sylvia, Margaret and the twenty-odd other women who collected Barbies. "And don't you all forget that I keep a rifle."

"Oh, Phyllis, that rifle is as old as the hills," Margaret said. "And you've never shot it in your life."

"I can start now."

Dan sighed. This was a bad idea. A very bad idea. "Fine. If you don't want to leave your Barbies here, then take them on home. I just can't guarantee they'll be safe."

"We all know who's taking them, Dan," Sylvia said. "So why don't you just arrest her?"

"What are you talking about, Sylvia?"

"That new girl. That Annie Jones. If that's her real name. The dolls showed up missing the day she came to town."

"There's no evidence that she had a thing to do with this."

"There's no evidence she didn't!"

"I'm not going to arrest her."

"Well, then, you just keep your eyes on her. Do whatever you have to. 'Cause sure as I'm standing here, she's the culprit."

Dan swiped his hand through his hair and

looked around for any of his deputies. The only one he saw was Sandy Kellog, but she was holding her own two Barbies close to her chest. What the hell was going on in this town? Had everyone gone crazy?

"That's right," Phyllis said. "You watch her like a hawk, Dan Collins. Never let her out of your sight."

"And how am I supposed to do that?"

"You'll think of something." Phyllis turned to the other women. "I, for one, am taking my girl home. And if you all know what's good for you, you'll take your girls home and lock 'em up. Let the sheriff do his job."

Phyllis led the way, and all the other women, except for Sandy Kellog, followed her out the door. Dan just watched. He kept thinking someone was going to jump out and tell him he was on *Candid Camera.*

"I'll leave my dolls here, Dan."

He turned to Sandy. "Great."

"But I think you'd better do what they said."

"Sandy, Annie Jones isn't stealing Barbies."

"How do you know?"

He walked over to his desk and sat down. His coffee had grown cold. It didn't matter. He drank it anyway. "I know because I've talked to her."

"And?"

"And I just know, that's all."

"She's real pretty."

"What does that have to do with anything?"

"I'm just saying that sometimes a pretty face can lie the best."

"Tell you what," Dan said. "I'm going to try and do some work. Real work. Sheriff's work. Let's see if you can do some deputy work."

"You can be as grouchy as you like," she said, walking past him to the dispatcher's office. "But I'd hate to be you if one more Barbie gets stolen."

"I'd hate to be me right now," he said under his breath. The whole day had gone to hell in a handbasket. First the story had come out in the local paper, then the phones had started ringing. He'd come up with the brilliant idea to store the Barbies here, and then the newspeople had begun to arrive. He'd kept them at bay, but that was only temporary. They were all waiting outside like vultures.

Now everyone was gunning for Annie, who he knew couldn't be guilty. At least he thought so. But what if he was wrong? No. He wasn't. He might not have the greatest judgment in the world when it came to women, but damn it, he knew thieves. And Annie wasn't one.

ANNIE SAW the crowd as soon as she turned the corner. A whole big group of women, carrying something. She walked toward them and then she saw what they had. Barbies. In boxes. Probably some kind of club. They certainly looked like they were having fun.

"Morning, Annie."

She recognized the woman from the fund-raiser. Sylvia. That's right. "Morning."

"Isn't it a lovely day today?" Sylvia said, and then she giggled.

Annie got a funny feeling in her stomach. "Yes, it is."

"And where might you be off to?" an older woman said.

"I was just taking a walk," Annie said, clutching her purse tightly, even though the idea that this group of women could be a gang was absurd.

"To the sheriff's department, perhaps?"

Now she was really getting nervous. "Well, yes, actually. I was."

"That Dan Collins is one mighty nice-looking young man," someone said. Annie couldn't tell who.

"And he's a good boy," the older woman chimed in. "You could do a lot worse."

"Now, I heard somewhere that you're something of a cook, is that so?"

Surprised, Annie looked at a woman she'd not seen before, elderly, with white, tightly curled hair. "Well, um, I can cook, but I'm no gourmet."

"Hmm. Well, that's a start. And you're a teacher, eh?"

Annie nodded.

"Good, good. That means you like children."

Annie maneuvered herself slowly. She edged her way around the women, taking little steps. No quick movements. But as soon as she had a clear shot, she began to back away, smiling all the while. "Yes, yes, I do," she said. "But darn, look at the time. I really have to be going now. Nice meeting you."

"He likes ribs," someone said.

"And horses."

"And mystery novels."

"Don't forget rodeo. He's a nut for rodeos."

"Peach pie."

Annie just kept nodding. Smiling. Backing away. Five more feet, and then she turned to make her getaway. Laughter followed her down the street. When she risked a look back, she saw the gang of women hadn't moved. They were all standing there watching her, their Barbies held close to their chests. She waved, then ducked inside the first doorway that was open.

She hummed the *Twilight Zone* theme song to herself as she looked around. It was a hardware store, which was a happy coincidence. She needed to get some picture hangers and a drain stop. As she walked down the aisles, she tried to shake off the weird feeling the encounter had given her, but it wasn't easy. Crazy, just crazy.

Why were they all so interested in her? And why were they so intent on getting her together with Dan? Maybe it had something to do with small towns that she just didn't understand.

On the other hand, maybe there was something fishy about Dan Collins. Maybe they didn't want a local girl getting stuck with him. He'd been married before. What had happened to his ex-wife? Was there something sinister going on?

"Hey."

Annie jumped at the voice, dropping her purse.

A man she recognized from the barbecue bent and picked it up. "Sorry, didn't mean to startle you."

"That's okay. I'm just a little jumpy."

"Frank Collins. We met at Reese's."

"I remember. How are you?"

"Just fine. Can I help you?"

She took back her purse. "I'm just picking up a couple of things," she said. "Thanks."

"No problem."

Annie smiled. At least he was normal. Good-looking, too, but not anywhere near Dan's league.

"You let me know if I can be of service," Frank said.

She nodded, then turned to go. As she hit the end of the aisle, Frank said, "Dan's real good with kids, you know."

Annie didn't know what to say. She just nodded and moved on over to the door locks. She picked out the biggest, sturdiest dead bolt she could find.

SHE HEARD HIM next door. What harm would it do just to ask? The man had to eat, and so did she. It wouldn't mean a thing if they did it together. She was just being neighborly. She couldn't possibly eat the whole lasagna herself.

It had been three days since she'd seen Dan. Three interesting, bewildering days. She'd met quite a few people in her explorations, but most of them either talked about Dan, or quizzed her on her homemaking skills.

She'd thought about talking to Dan about the situation, but she didn't know how to bring it up. So maybe it was a good idea to just ask him over. Sound him out about things.

It was clear there was matchmaking going on, but it wasn't normal. It wasn't natural. It was almost as though they had to convince her that Dan was someone she should like. A whole town full of used-car salesmen, except this wasn't just an automobile, and she didn't like the idea of being stuck with a lemon. Yet she didn't think Dan was a lemon. He seemed so nice. His smile was so genuine. And the way he blushed made her toes curl.

On the other hand, she barely knew him. Maybe there was a deep, dark secret to Dan, one the whole town knew about, but no one would admit. She'd once gone out with a guy who liked to wear women's underwear. That had certainly taken her by surprise. So maybe Dan was into something a little bit kinky? It didn't seem likely, but she was no expert.

Face it, she didn't have much experience with men. The guys she'd gone with had been convenient. They'd asked. She'd said yes. But when it was over, she hadn't shed any tears. When it came to romance, she was a rookie, plain and simple. But that didn't mean she didn't have instincts. And her instincts about Dan were all positive.

The timer buzzed and she went to the kitchen and turned off the oven. It was Friday night, and she was dressed for company already. So what the heck?

After a quick check in the mirror to make sure there hadn't been a makeup mistake, she went to the door. But just as she was about to reach for the knob, someone knocked.

For the second time that day she jumped, startled out of her wits. With a thudding heart, she turned the dead bolt, but didn't open the door just yet. "Who is it?"

"Dan."

She swung the door open. He stood in the hallway and once more his size took her breath away. His worn jeans and button-down cowboy shirt fit his body perfectly. His dark hair was slightly mussed and a little damp around the edges.

She felt her insides go all mushy, and she squeezed her legs together tightly for a second.

"Evening," he said.

"Hi."

"I was just thinking about going out for a bite. Thought if you weren't doing anything…"

"What a happy coincidence. I was just coming over to your place to invite you to dinner."

"Really?"

She nodded. "I've got lasagna and salad. Nothing special."

"Homemade lasagna? That's special, all right."

"Great, so come on in."

"Hold on, I'll be right back."

She took the opportunity to let her gaze linger on his backside as he went to his apartment. It was a very nice backside. A tight end, as Rachel would say. He came back to the hall a moment later carrying a bottle of wine.

"Some Chianti," he said. "Okay?"

She smiled, and held the door open for him.

He changed the room. Changed the proportions of the space itself. Her couch seemed smaller, so did the chairs. Yet he didn't seem out of place. On the contrary. He looked like he'd always belonged with her things.

"I read about you in the paper," she said.

Dan groaned. "Don't get me started."

"Caught some flack, did you?"

"You have no idea." He put the wine down on the dining-room table, then turned to her. "Tell you what. Let's try and have a whole evening where the subject of Barbies never comes up."

She laughed. "Deal."

"Thank you."

"Sit," she said. "Everything's ready."

He pulled out a chair and sighed as he sat. He seemed comfortable, which pleased her for some reason. She wanted him to like her food, to like her place. Frankly, she wanted him to like her.

"How was your day?" he asked.

"Fine. But I'm ready to get to work."

"When do you start?"

"Monday. But I went in a few days this week to get everything ready."

"Great. I'll bet you're a hell of a teacher."

"I like to think so."

"Did you paint those pictures in the living room?"

She'd put them up yesterday afternoon. Three of her favorites. All three of them were landscapes. Gardens. "Yes, I did."

"You're very good."

"Thank you."

"I mean it."

It shouldn't have meant so much to her, but his compliment pleased her deeply. She brought the salad to the table, then went back for the lasagna. Finally, she was sitting across from him, and she was serving him salad while he opened the wine. For the first time since she'd come to Harlen, she felt as though she were home.

"Tell me about you," she said.

"Nothing much to tell," he said, pouring her a glass of Chianti. "I've lived here all my life. Followed in my father's footsteps."

"But you were in the rodeo. You were married."

His brow came down with that last comment, and she wondered again at the mystery surrounding Dan Collins. "Neither of which would interest you."

"Why don't you let me be the judge of that?"

He stared at her for a long while. She could almost hear the gears in his head cranking as he decided what to tell her. She hoped he'd opt for honesty. The way she was feeling about him, she needed to know the truth.

"I imagine you want to hear about the marriage, and not the rodeo?"

She nodded. But she didn't press. Instead, she served them both, then began to eat, all the while watching him. She almost told him to forget it. But something urged her to be silent even though it made him uncomfortable.

"This is good," he said.

"Thanks."

He took another bite, chewed thoughtfully, then sipped some wine. "I met her in high school," he said. "She was the most beautiful girl I'd ever seen. She came from Six Trees, which is a town about fifty miles from here. Smaller, even, than Harlen. She had long, dark hair. Tiny thing, not even five foot three. But she had so much energy. A regular dynamo. I think I loved her from that first day."

Annie put her fork down.

"We got married too soon, I think. I'd just graduated from college, but I still had to go to the academy. Melissa didn't want to work, so she stayed home. It was real good for a while. But then, she started getting restless. I guess it didn't help that I was gone so much. She had to spend a lot of time by herself. I was trying to make something of myself. I thought that's what we agreed to. Anyway, she wasn't happy with some things, I guess, 'cause she started making changes. She got her teeth bonded, and her nose fixed, although I swear there wasn't a thing wrong with the old nose. Then she had some implants. I didn't want her to, but I figured she needed to feel pretty, so I kept quiet."

"It must have been expensive."

"I worked two jobs for a while. Saw her even less. But I wanted her to be happy."

"And?"

"And she got happy, all right. Felt pretty, too. But then she still needed to change one more thing. Her husband."

"Ouch."

"She ended up marrying her divorce lawyer. An old friend of ours from high school."

"Wow, that must have been awful."

He studied his plate for a moment. "He was my closest friend. I introduced him to Melissa. He was the best man at our wedding."

"I'm sorry."

"Wasn't your fault."

"I'm not apologizing. I'm sympathizing."

"Don't bother. It's over and done with."

"Well, I'm sorry nonetheless. Thank you for telling me."

"Don't know why it matters," he said, busying himself with the garlic toast. "It's ancient history."

"It matters because it's part of you. Part of who you are."

He grew still again. "Why do you care, Annie?"

She didn't answer right away. She thought of not answering at all. But he'd been honest with her, even though it had been hard. She owed him the same. "I care because I like you, Dan. Because I'm hoping to know you better."

"I'd advise against it."

"Too late."

"I'm not looking for that, Annie. I told you."

Annie had to decide. Part of her wanted to let it go. To play it safe. To finish her lasagna and go on with her boring, predictable life. But another part of her wanted to risk it. To throw caution to the wind, and to listen to her body instead of her head. It was now or never.

Let it be now.

"What if I told you I'm not looking for that, either?" she said quietly.

His brows come down, and he leaned forward. "Then what?"

She took in a deep breath. In for a penny, in for a pound. "I'm not sure, but I think what I want is a lover. A temporary lover."

9

DAN DIDN'T THINK he'd heard right. He couldn't have. "You want a lover? A temporary lover?"

He watched as Annie's blush started in her cheeks then spread until her whole face was a very becoming shade of pink. "Oh, heavens," she said. "I can't believe I said that. Forget it, would you? Just chalk it up to summer dementia."

She stood up, clearly anxious to run, but he took hold of her hand and held her steady. "I don't think I can forget it," he said. "So why don't we talk about it?"

She squirmed a little, then calmed down, but she wouldn't look at him. "God, I sound like the Whore of Babylon. I don't say things like that, honest. Ever. I'm normally a very shy person. I don't know you well enough to ask... To imply... Oh, just shoot me."

He laughed. "Sit down, Annie."

She did, but he didn't let go of her hand.

"Can't you just pretend you didn't hear me? I won't be here long. Just a couple of months. I promise never to bother you again."

"Annie. I'm not bothered. On the contrary. I'm quite flattered."

"Flattered. Right." She still wouldn't meet his gaze.

"And if you can get past the embarrassment, I'd like to know if you meant it."

Now she looked. Her eyes were wide, her gaze frightened. He knew she'd been telling the truth when she said this wasn't her normal behavior. But that just made it all the more enticing.

The truth was he wanted her to mean it. Wanted it badly. Ever since he'd walked into her apartment he'd been captivated by her. The way she looked in her sundress, the way she smelled like flowers. The way she moved, and talked and listened.

Wanting Annie Jones was unlike anything he'd experienced before. But having her?

Despite her words, he didn't believe that Annie wanted something as fleeting as a temporary lover. She just wasn't the type. How he knew that wasn't clear to him, but it was true nonetheless. If Annie fell, it would be like a brick, not a feather. Once she loved, it would be with all her heart.

He could see she wasn't going to answer him. Not straight out. "Here's what I think," he said, softly. "I think you *like* the idea of a temporary lover, but in practice, you're not so sure."

She gave a little nod. "I just can't believe I actually said it out loud. My sister—now, she would have said that. Not me."

"But you did. And I'm glad. Because you're all I've thought about for days."

"Really?"

He nodded. "You're an incredibly beautiful woman. I think I was a goner from the first moment I laid eyes on you, that day at the picnic."

"But—" she swallowed, then took a deep breath "—but you don't want to get involved."

Now it was his turn to look away. "I can't deny that. I'm not looking for marriage, it's true. But that doesn't mean we can't..."

"Sleep together."

He smiled. "I was going to say 'date.' But then I'm not as brave as you."

"Brave? Or stupid?"

"Brave. Definitely. After all, you're the one that came to town not knowing a soul. You're the one living out a longtime dream. And, God knows, you've certainly learned to say what you mean."

"That's a nice way of putting it."

He moved his other hand to the table, capturing both of her hands. She was so small, so delicate. Like a perfect doll. Anatomically correct, of course. He laughed.

"What?"

"Nothing. I just like the way you feel, that's all."

She looked at his hands. "Dan, you don't have to do this. I was out of line, and I didn't mean to put you on the spot."

"You haven't." He reached over and brushed her cheek with the back of his hand. "To tell you the truth, I was planning to seduce you."

Her gaze came back to his. "You were?"

"Yep. Right after dinner."

"Oh, yeah. I kind of interrupted dinner, didn't I?"

"Not a problem."

"I have dessert, you know. Peach pie."

"I'm not hungry, but thank you."

"You're welcome."

Her eyes hadn't wavered. And the longer she looked at him, the more he became aware of the rest of his body. The tightness of his chest, the feel of her silky soft hand, the need that pressed against his jeans.

He stood up, and pulled her up beside him.

"Where are we going?"

He didn't tell her. He showed her. Walking slowly, keeping her very close, he moved into the living room. To the long couch. But he didn't let her sit. He couldn't. Not until he'd done what he'd wanted to do since the first time he'd seen her.

He kissed her.

The moment his lips touched hers, he knew he couldn't turn back. The softness of her was like a dream, the taste of her beyond words. He felt her tongue tentatively touch his, and that was it. He let go. Abandoned himself to the sensations that were causing havoc all through his body. He used his mouth to tell her of his need, and she responded by melting into his arms.

Breaking away for a moment, he sat on the

couch, then pulled her close. She fit snugly next to him, as if she belonged there. He looked into those big green eyes, and damned if he didn't see desire in her gaze. The same desire that urged him to touch her shiny hair. To explore her pale skin.

He moaned as his lips touched hers once more. Kissing Annie did something strange to his solar plexus. He felt tight and hot and strong. He could do anything, scale the tallest building, ride the wildest horse. Yet he touched her shoulder with just his fingertips, so very aware of how delicate she was.

Annie shivered as Dan's fingers traced her shoulder. She felt her whole body respond to his soft touch. So big, so gentle, it didn't seem possible, but there it was.

And his kiss...

My lord, she hadn't realized kissing could be like this. The men she'd been with before had been gauche, almost swallowing her whole. This, this was an entirely different thing. She'd never again think of those previous experiences as kissing. Not now. Not when she finally understood what kissing was supposed to feel like.

His mouth, his lips, his tongue—perfect, hot, moist. Tasting, teasing, making her moan. She wanted to stay like this forever.

Turning more toward him, she put her right hand on his chest. Another miracle. She'd heard people say that men built like Dan were solid as rocks, but this was no stone. There was heat beneath her palm, flesh under his T-shirt, and if she held very still, she could feel his heartbeat.

"Annie," he whispered.

She looked up, meeting his gaze. "Yes?" she said, her voice soft and breathless.

"I'd better warn you. Another minute, and I won't want to leave."

The disappointment was a physical blow. "Do you? Want to leave, I mean?"

"No. But I want you to be sure."

She knew it was up to her. If she took a chance and asked him to stay, they would make love. If she behaved as usual, she'd tell him to go. But something else was happening here, something she hadn't counted on. She'd never been drawn to a man like this before. Never in her life. Frankly, she hadn't known what all the fuss was about. She'd made love, but no bells had rung and the earth certainly hadn't moved.

Her body had never responded like this to a kiss. She felt more like a woman than she ever had before, and the need to be with him was as real as the couch they were sitting on. If she let him go, would she regret it?

This was her chance. Her chance to be daring, to live her life instead of just standing in the shadows. Rachel would tell her to take him to bed. To be courageous for once. To let herself be happy.

She had no idea if she was making the biggest mistake of her life, but if she was, she'd accept the consequences. Because letting him walk out that door would break something inside of her. She had the awful feeling the break would be permanent.

She stood, studying the man in front of her. His expression held all the concern in the world. But his eyes, they were pure desire. She held her hand out, and after a moment, he took it. He stood, and she felt most grateful for the gentle squeeze he gave her.

"Are you sure?" he whispered.

She nodded. Then she smiled, and led him toward the bedroom.

He pulled her to a stop as they reached the door. "Wait," he said.

Her throat tightened. He didn't want her. She'd read him all wrong. Oh, Lord, she couldn't even look at him.

"Do you have protection?" he asked.

She laughed with relief, then sobered quickly as she realized the importance of his question. "Oh, no."

He smiled at her. "Wait right here. I'll be two seconds."

He hurried out, slamming her door in his haste.

Was she really doing this? Taking this man to her bed? With every other man in her life, she'd waited. Waited until they'd known each other a very proper length of time. It hadn't been difficult. But she'd never *wanted* like this before. Now, the idea of waiting, just these few seconds while he went next door, was like torture.

Maybe she should go to her bedroom. Undress quickly, and get into bed. Fluff the pillows and spread her hair out like she'd seen in the movies. But then he wouldn't see her underwear.

No, she'd bought these for the express purpose of showing them off. It occurred to her that as she'd picked them out, she'd been thinking of Dan.

The decision was made for her as Dan rushed back inside. He shut the door behind him and turned the lock. She was a little surprised at the handful of little packages he'd brought back. "Wow," she said. "You're quite optimistic."

He laughed as he took her hand and continued the walk to the bedroom. "I was a Boy Scout," he said.

Once in her room, Dan put the condoms on her night table, then he turned to look at her once more, but he wasn't laughing. "You're sure?"

"If you keep asking me that, I'm going to start thinking you don't want to."

He shook his head. "You'd be wrong. Really wrong."

"Okay then," she said.

He sat down on her bed, but he didn't move to take off his T-shirt or jeans. He just looked at her.

"What?" she asked.

"I want to see that underwear you talk so much about."

She felt her cheeks heat, remembering what she'd blurted out at the restaurant. But her embarrassment was short-lived. With a bravado that she didn't know she had, she stood in front of him, and reached for the bottom of her dress. Lifting it slowly, she raised the hem over her thighs, then higher. She watched him watch her, and if she lived to be a hundred, she doubted she'd ever feel quite this sexy again.

His eyes grew wider as she continued her impromptu striptease. First, she revealed her panties. They were white, but not the white of her old cotton underwear. These shimmered and hugged her like a second skin.

She lifted the dress higher, holding her stomach in. She wanted him to like what he saw. Not just the underwear, but what was underneath that. While she kept in pretty good shape, she knew her flaws all too well. But looking at him, she had the feeling he wasn't noticing them.

She pulled the dress up all the way over her head, then tossed it on the dresser.

There. She stood in the middle of her room, in this little demi-bra and panties that were more Victoria's Secret than JCPenney. His gaze lingered over each part of her, and to her delight, she wasn't ashamed.

"You're incredible," he said, his voice much lower than it had been a moment ago.

"Thank you," she said, feeling his compliment

all the way down to her toes. "Now it's your turn."

"I don't have new underwear."

"It's new to me."

He smiled as he started tugging his T-shirt out of his jeans.

"Oh, no. Not like that." She took his hands and pulled him up, then quickly sat down on the bed.

"You want me to strip for you?"

She nodded. "It's only fair."

"But I don't look as good as you."

"I'll be the judge of that."

"Whatever the lady wants," he said.

Annie couldn't help but laugh as she watched Dan perform what had to be the fastest striptease of all time. His T-shirt was off in a snap, his boots came next, and then his jeans, and before she had a chance to get a good look at him, he was down to his shorts. Boxers. She liked boxers.

"Voilà," he said, holding his arms straight out. "I told you I didn't have great underwear."

"But yours do tricks," she said.

He looked down and laughed. "He's just happy to see you, I guess," he said. "Very happy."

"I see," she said.

Dan looked at her again, and his smile faded. His arms came down slowly as he moved toward her.

She had only a moment to take him all in. He was more magnificent than she'd imagined. His chest was muscled perfectly, dusted with dark hair that came to a V just past his rippled belly. His legs were long and strong, his hips narrow and tight. "You're beautiful," she said, as his legs touched the side of the bed.

"No, you are," he whispered. Then he leaned down, and took her face in his hands. His kiss stole her breath away. Her eyes fluttered closed as she tasted him again, as she nibbled his lower lip. She didn't open them again until he pulled back. He'd gone to his knees in front of her, and now he took hold of her thighs and spread them apart. He nestled between them, and she wrapped her legs around him.

Slowly, reverently, his hands moved up her thighs, up her tummy, until they reached her breasts. He cupped them gently, then with a magician's grace he unhooked the clasp of her bra. She heard his sharp intake of breath as he peeled the material back, leaving her bare. She didn't have to look down to know that her nipples were hard. It was far more interesting to watch him. To see how his eyes darkened, how his breath grew shallow. And then when he leaned over and kissed her there, tasted her, suckled her, she didn't want to see anything. Just feel.

His gentle ministrations made her moan, and without conscious thought her hands moved to his head, holding him steady as he teased her flesh with his tongue. A fire started deep in her belly, and in a heartbeat it was raging out of control.

She gasped when he pulled back, when he took her wrists in his hands and put them down on the bed. Then he surprised her again by gently coaxing her to lie down. She didn't understand at first. But then she felt his fingers tug on her panties. She didn't even have to lift up. A moment later, she was naked before him.

He kissed her then, on the delicate flesh of her inner thigh. She felt his hot breath, his moist tongue, as he moved toward her center.

She knew what he was going to do, and she felt her heart thunder in her chest. No one had ever... She'd never dared to ask. She closed her eyes, and gripped her bedspread tight.

First, he touched her ever so lightly with his fingers. A shiver ran through her, but it didn't stop. He lingered there, teasing, brushing her lightly over and over. She continued to tremble as she felt his breath, followed by his mouth, and then there was nothing but fire and torment and moaning and pleasure beyond anything she'd ever known. He didn't let up, only increased the pressure, already knowing her body better than she did. She climbed and climbed, and just when she thought she couldn't go any higher, he pushed her over the edge.

She heard her own cries, and she was helpless to stop them. She trembled and keened and bucked beneath him. It felt as if a million volts of electricity were wracking her body.

Even as she trembled, she felt him next to her, lifting her and moving her up on the bed. Dimly she heard him tear open a package, then she opened her eyes to see him above her, his beautiful face filled with a desire so keen she could feel it in her chest. He settled between her legs, and in one slow, deliberate motion, he thrust himself inside her.

She wrapped her legs around his back and found his rhythm. She heard him call her name, over and over. She let herself go, let herself drown in the pleasure as her body once more began the climb.

He filled her completely, yet it didn't hurt at all. She was made to hold him, to please him. His muscles grew taut, his thrusts faster.

And then he called her name and she let go. Trembling, crying in his embrace as he came inside her. Reaching up to his neck and pulling him into a kiss that was sex and release all in one.

She quivered for a long time. After the kiss, after his sigh, after he lay beside her with his arms around her. Finally, finally, she settled into a sweet, satisfied calm.

10

DAN LISTENED to Annie's slow, even breathing. He thought about getting up, but her head was resting on his arm and he didn't want to disturb her. He could ignore the fact that his arm was falling asleep, but he couldn't avoid the realization that something had happened to him in the last few hours. Something he hadn't counted on.

All this time, he'd thought he could find someone who just wanted to have sex, and that would be that. He must have found the wrong someone.

The terrible truth was that he hadn't had sex with Annie. He'd made love. *Love*. The last thing in the world he'd wanted or needed. Yet making her happy, hearing her cry out, holding her in his arms had affected his heart, not just his less discriminating body parts. Damn it. This was not supposed to happen.

Now what was he going to do? If he left now, there was still a chance he could get out of this with no permanent damage. On the other hand, the thought of leaving her was totally unacceptable. He wanted to be there when she woke up. He wanted to talk to her, listen to her. He wanted to make love to her again.

So where did that leave him? With a very big problem, that's where.

He dared another look at her, knowing it was a mistake. Lord, but she was beautiful. Her hair was tousled and sexy. Her skin so smooth and soft it was as if she was made from finer stuff than flesh. Spun from silk, maybe. The sheet only covered her to her waist, and he let his gaze wander down her body. Perfect. Just perfect. Her breasts weren't very large, but they suited her. They suited him.

He sighed and she moved, releasing his arm. He lifted it to get the circulation going again, careful not to disturb her further.

Looking at the bedside clock, he was shocked to find that it was after 3:00 a.m. The night had gone by in a flash. He should be sleeping. Thank goodness he didn't have to go to work until Monday. He'd need the time to recover.

"Are you okay?"

He looked back at Annie. Her eyes were barely open, her voice gravelly from sleep.

"Hush, go back to sleep. I'm fine."

"Dan?"

"Yeah?" he said, whispering.

"Did I say thanks?"

"Yeah, honey. You did."

"Good." Then she closed her eyes once more, and tucked a fist under her chin. An instant later, she was asleep.

"Thank *you*," he said. "I think." He yawned

and scrunched down, turning so he could put his arm around her waist. Moving so the front of his legs touched the back of hers. Then he, too, closed his eyes.

COFFEE WOKE HER. The delicious scent began in her dream, then drifted into reality when she opened her eyes. Dan. He'd been in her dream, too. She couldn't remember the specifics, but she knew it had been sweet.

"You're already awake."

She looked up to see him standing at the door. He had his boxers on, and once again she was simply awed by his physique. His chest alone deserved a medal.

"I wasn't sure how you liked your coffee."

Only then did she notice the cup in his hand. "I'm afraid I'm not very macho when it comes to coffee," she said, adjusting the pillows behind her and sitting up, tucking the sheet around her chest. "I take it with sugar and cream."

"That's good," he said, walking toward her. "'Cause that's how I fixed it."

"Well, aren't you intuitive?"

"Not really," he said, grinning. "I saw the flavored cream in the fridge and the sugar canister right next to the coffee."

"Well, if not intuitive, then, at the very least, attentive. But I already knew that."

He handed her the mug, then sat down next to her on the bed. "Oh?"

"Uh-huh. It was your attention to detail that got me."

"And what would you be referring to, Miss?"

"You know exactly what I'm talking about."

He feigned a look of bewilderment, and she laughed. Which wasn't such a bright move, as a drop of coffee spilled right onto her chest, just above the sheet. "Ouch."

"You okay?"

She nodded. "That'll teach me to lounge around in my birthday suit."

"I like the look," he said. "Very much."

"But it's dangerous."

"That's true."

She smiled. Sipped her coffee. Took tremendous pleasure in the fact that Dan's hand was on her thigh. It was hard to believe it was reality, and not still part of the dream.

"So, I was thinking..." he said.

"Yes?"

"I was thinking I should go next door and feed Cougar."

"Your dog, I assume?"

He nodded.

"I don't for a moment want him to be hungry, but I was thinking something else, too."

"Oh?"

"About a shower."

"Together?"

She smiled.

"Cougar can wait."

"Oh, goody." She took another sip of coffee, then put the mug on the nightstand. With only a little twinge of self-consciousness, she slipped out from under the sheet and stood up.

Dan stood too, and he caught her right hand in his, and pulled her close.

"I have to brush my teeth," she said, trying to avoid breathing in his face.

"I can take it." He leaned down and kissed her gently on the lips. Then on each cheek.

She sighed happily, then pulled him toward the bathroom. "You can get the towels out of the cupboard," she said, pointing to the linen closet, "while I take care of a few details."

He went to do as she asked, and she hurried to the bathroom. It only took her a few moments to finish her business, and then she opened the door. He was standing right there. "Ready, are you?"

"Willing and able, too."

She let him come inside, and she turned on the shower. It wasn't big. Just a regular bathtub setup with a purple-and-pink plastic curtain. But the water pressure was good. She stepped inside, and he followed. At least she wasn't the only one in her birthday suit.

She looked down and smiled. "I see what you mean about the willing-and-able part."

He didn't respond. Instead, he got the washcloth and the soap and lathered it up. "Turn," he said.

She obeyed. He began to wash her back, and

there was no way to keep her eyes open or to keep silent. It was too wonderful. She moaned, feeling her muscles relax, her mind drift into the pleasure zone. It got more interesting the lower he went. One thing she was learning about Dan Collins. He certainly was thorough.

"Turn," he said again.

She did, already anticipating the feel of the soap and his hand on her skin. He didn't disappoint. The more he rubbed, the more she ached. She hadn't realized she had so much patience. But she wasn't going to hurry him. Not when it felt so good to feel him rub her *right there*.

She shifted a bit, expecting him to move down to her legs, but he didn't. What he did do was drop the washcloth. She started to shake, and she leaned back against the cold tile. It wasn't clear to her if the jolt had come from the contact with the cold surface, or from his magic fingers.

All she knew was that he was giving her more pleasure than she'd thought possible. No one had ever taken such care of her. She could get used to this.

"Feel good?" he asked.

"Oh, yeah," she said.

"How about this?" he asked, as he moved his fingers inside her.

"Oh, Dan. Oh, please."

"Please what?"

"That. Do that more."

"This?"

She nodded. Then she grabbed on to his shoulders, and there was no more talking.

BY THE TIME Dan got back from feeding the dog, breakfast was all laid out. Not in the kitchen, however. Annie had brought two trays and set them on the bed. She'd made scrambled eggs, bacon, toast, orange juice and brought the rest of the coffee. She also hadn't dressed.

He'd slipped on his jeans to go next door, but now that he understood the dress code, he took them off again. This was going to be a very, very good weekend.

He still hadn't fully recovered from the shower. Annie had said thank you again, only this time she'd shown her gratitude in a most incredible way. They'd used up all the hot water, but damn, it was for a worthy cause.

"I can't remember when I've been this hungry," she said, taking a big bite of toast.

"Exercise will do that to you."

"I work out," she mumbled. "This is different."

He got himself situated cross-legged beside her, then dug into his eggs. They were perfect. Just like Annie.

For a few moments, all they did was take care of their immediate need for food. Eventually, the desperation subsided, and they could sip coffee at a more leisurely pace.

"Talk to me, Annie Jones. Tell me how in the world you ended up in Harlen."

She smiled. "I told you already."

"Rachel, right?"

"Uh-huh. She's the one that got me here. If I hadn't come, she wouldn't have taken her summer job, and then she wouldn't have tuition for next year."

"So basically you're saying that you're here against your will?"

"No. Not really. Rachel's blackmail was more of a catalyst than anything else. She's known for a long time that I wanted to teach art, and that I wanted to try living in a small town. I just needed a little push."

"You two are close, then?"

Annie nodded. "Very. My folks are gone, so it's just the two of us. I pretty much raised her from the time she was fourteen."

"Big responsibility."

"You have no idea. Rachel is a handful."

"How old is she?"

"Twenty."

He was surprised. "And you're still taking care of her?"

Annie studied her orange juice. "I know, she should be on her own, but you don't know Rachel. She has this uncanny ability to get herself into trouble. She needs me."

"And you?"

She looked up. "Hmm?"

"Who do you need?"

She didn't answer him. Which was a kind of an answer in itself.

"Are you through?" Annie said, moving to the edge of the bed. "More coffee maybe?"

"No, I'm fine," he said. "But tell me something. What would happen if you stayed here after the summer?"

She shook her head, a little too vigorously. "Not possible. Rachel has to start school. I have to work. I'm just here for the summer, that's all. Then I have to go back to the real world."

"This isn't real to you?" He could tell she didn't want to have this conversation, but he didn't care. He'd screwed up before by not getting all the facts before he acted. This time, there were not going to be any surprises.

"Of course it's real. It's better than real." She reached over and took his hand. "I haven't even started my job, but I know I'm going to love it. And you... Who ever expected you?"

He rubbed the inside of her palm with his thumb and took a moment to look at her. He felt compelled to memorize her, to store the information where he could get it whenever he needed to.

"What are you smiling about?" she asked.

"I didn't realize I was."

"It's a very nice smile."

"I'll try to remember that."

"Good." She extricated her hand, then stood up and collected one of the trays.

Dan watched her walk to the door, stirring at

the sight of her body, her behind with the two symmetrical dimples on each cheek.

When he was alone, he put the second tray on the nightstand, then crawled under the sheet to wait for Annie's return. He pondered getting dressed. Leaving. He needed to change the oil in his truck. Take Cougar to the park. Do laundry. But he dismissed the whole list. It wasn't very wise, but he was going to stay with Annie as long as she'd let him.

He kept thinking about what she'd said—how she couldn't possibly stay in Harlen past the summer. That should have been very welcome news. A guarantee that neither of them were going to make any serious mistakes, like falling in love, or wanting to get married. He absolutely didn't want to do either of those things. And yet...

The thing was, he felt good. Really good. He hadn't felt this way in a long, long time. Only one thing in his life had changed. And she was walking toward him, naked, wearing just a hint of a wicked grin.

ANNIE COULDN'T believe how exhausted she felt. Or how wonderful. The day had flown by, and neither she nor Dan had gotten out of bed. Of course, they hadn't made love the whole time. Just a good portion of the time. She'd finally had to cry uncle. At least for now.

He'd gone over to his apartment to shower and change, and she was doing the same. In only a half hour, he expected her knock on his door. Right now, the problem was choosing something to wear.

Annie stared at her clothes, but her gaze kept wandering back to her jeans. Maybe a dress would be better. No, jeans and a top would be fine. She plucked one of her favorite blouses, a short-sleeved, silky, blue-striped number, and her Levi's and tossed them on the bed. Then she went to her underwear drawer. How grateful she was that she'd indulged herself at Victoria's Secret. Tonight, she'd go for pink. She laughed when she realized the whole time she'd been choosing her wardrobe, she'd been humming "I Enjoy Being A Girl." How silly. How true.

She tried to think of the last time she'd had so much fun, or felt so much passion. But none of her past relationships had ever been like this. She'd known Jerry longer, actually, she'd known each of the three men she'd dated seriously longer than she'd known Dan. It was crazy. It couldn't happen this fast, could it?

She tossed her towel on the bed and slipped on her pink undies. Then she went back to the bathroom for the hair and makeup portion of the evening. When she looked at herself in the mirror, she was surprised to see the same old Annie staring back. She'd thought she would have changed, somehow.

As she went through her routine, she thought about what she was going to tell Rachel. Her first impulse was to tell her all. To let her sister know that she wasn't a complete washout in the men department. Rachel might not take it that way, though. She'd probably give herself all the credit.

So what? Let Rachel gloat. She had been right. Dan Collins was even better in person than he sounded on paper. The ad hadn't mentioned the sound of his laughter. The way he looked when he slept. How he made her go crazy, with just a touch.

If only it could last. No. She wouldn't think about that. Maybe it was only for a summer, and maybe it would hurt like hell when it ended, but she didn't have to start feeling bad yet, did she? Why jump the gun? For now, all she had to do was let go. Let her heart keep leading her forward. It had worked like a charm last night.

Imagine, Professor Annie Jones, a wanton femme fatale. Whatever would they think back at the sociology department? She laughed, then caught sight of her clock. Whoa, she was gonna be late.

"GINA, Annie didn't steal your Barbies."

"How do you know?"

"Because I've been with her all weekend." Dan sat down on the couch, and tried to control his temper. He'd heard enough about stolen dolls to last a lifetime. Annie was due any second, and he didn't want her to hear about this latest theft. At least not from him. He'd already practically accused her, and this time, he knew for a fact that she was innocent.

"I don't know, Dan. I found out the Barbies were missing today, but who knows when they were stolen?"

He didn't need this. "When did you last see them?"

"Wednesday afternoon," Gina said, sniffling. "Right after lunch."

"And where were they?"

"In the back room, in the cabinet."

"Was the cabinet locked?"

"No. But the house was locked. Shouldn't that have been enough?"

"It should have. Are you sure you didn't see them before Friday night?"

"I'm sure. They had to have been stolen Thursday. That was the only time no one was here."

"I'll have Logan come on by. He'll check it out."

"Okay," Gina said. "But I have to tell you. I saw that new girl wandering around on Thursday, just before I left to go to Margaret's."

"I'll look into it, Gina."

"Okay," she said. "You do know that those dolls represent my life savings, don't you?"

Dan shook his head. "I'll find them for you. I promise."

"Thank you, Dan. Thank you."

Dan hung up the phone, and put his head in his hands. This Barbie business was going to be the end of him. He felt sure of that. How could he go out there and tell these people that he didn't consider Annie a suspect? When they asked him why, how could he tell them it was just a gut feeling? They'd call for his dismissal, that's what they'd do. Ride him out of town on a rail for sleeping with the prime suspect. Who knows? Maybe they'd be right.

11

ANNIE RAN her hand over her hair and pressed her lips together to make sure her lipstick was even before she knocked on Dan's door. It opened so quickly, she figured he must have been standing right there, waiting. This night just kept getting better.

"Hey," he said, standing aside to let her in.

"Hey, right back," she said, but her attention had already gone to the black Lab who was greeting her in a very enthusiastic manner. It was clear the dog was well trained, because he didn't jump up on her, or even touch her for that matter. Instead, he quivered all over, sort of danced in a little shuffle, whined and ducked his head up and down. She knew exactly how he felt.

She got down on her knees, very grateful that she had decided to go with the jeans, and let Cougar smell her hands a bit before she greeted him back. When she started scratching him behind the ears, his excitement got the better of him, and he licked her face. She laughed, delighted.

"I think you have a fan there," Dan said, moving over to the couch.

"It's mutual. Oh, Dan, he's a beauty." She

switched her attention to Cougar. "Aren't you, sweetie?"

Dan leaned forward, watching her. "You want a drink or something before we head out to dinner? I have beer. And soda."

"No, thanks."

"I'm starting to get jealous," he said.

She took Cougar's head in her hands. "I think your daddy wants me to pet him, too. What do you think?"

Cougar's tail went into overdrive, and she took that for a "yes."

She got up and went to the couch, then reached over and started scratching Dan's ears. He laughed. But then she stopped fooling around and held his head steady, met his gaze, and leaned in for a kiss. And then he got serious. She'd meant the kiss to be gentle, playful, but that was clearly not what Dan had in mind. She went with the flow.

He took her by the hips and pulled her down onto his lap, never once letting up on the firm, deepening pressure on her lips. When she was settled, she wrapped one arm around his neck and returned his welcome properly.

Finally, after who knew how long, she came up for air, took a moment to remember how to speak, then said, "Think we ought to go?"

He nodded, but he didn't make any effort to actually move.

"Think we ought to go now?"

He nodded again, searching her eyes, her face.

She frowned. "What's going on in that devious mind of yours?"

"That you haven't seen my bedroom yet."

She shifted a bit on his lap, feeling the impetus for his change of topic there. As she ran her hand down his chest, she enjoyed the fact that although he was wearing a polo shirt, she could visualize his chest in minute detail. "If I go to see your bedroom, we won't have dinner."

"I can whip up something here."

Annie sighed. "As lovely as that sounds, I have to confess that while the spirit is willing, the flesh is weak."

"You're sore, huh?"

She nodded.

"I could kiss it and make it better."

"You are incorrigible. But I have to admit, I like the way you think."

"Well?"

"Nope. But hold that thought. I may take you up on it. Later." She stood up and held her hand out for him. He took it, but he made her pull.

Once they were standing, Dan stole another kiss, a little one. Then he ushered her to the door. She turned back to look at Cougar, which was an error, as the dog was at attention, waiting for the signal that he could join them. He was so eager, it broke her heart. "Can't Cougar come with us?"

At the mention of his name, the dog started toward them, his tail whipping back and forth with great fervor.

"On't-day ention-may is-hay ame-nay."

"Huh?"

Dan sighed. "You mean to tell me you don't know pig latin?"

She shook her head. "Sorry."

"What do they teach you in those universities?" He leaned down until his mouth was right next to her ear. "Don't mention his name. He'll think he gets to go."

"Can't he?"

"The restaurant doesn't allow ogs-day."

"I got that one," she said. "But maybe afterward, we could take him for a w-a-l-k?"

Cougar lost it. He jumped up on Dan's chest and barked.

"Uh oh," Annie said. "He can spell?"

"Only a few words." Dan pushed Cougar down. "Sit."

The dog obeyed, but he still had that bright-eyed look that meant he wasn't understanding the complexity of the conversation.

Dan grabbed Annie's hand and rushed them out. Annie heard Cougar's plaintive cry as the door swung shut.

"Don't let him get to you," Dan said. "That dog has already been out today, for a very long walk. He'll get another one when we get back."

"Okay," she said. "But I think we should bring him a treat."

"Softie."

She smiled up at him. "Caring."

"Pushover."

"I guess so. At least with my next-door neighbors."

"Good. I like that in a woman." Dan took her hand in his, and led her out of the complex, down to his truck.

Annie felt so happy her feet barely touched the ground. This feeling was so new, so unexpected, that a small voice inside her said it couldn't be true. She'd never really believed that she could find someone like Dan, someone who made her physically ache to be near him. She just hadn't had much luck in the romance department in the past. But, it seemed, her luck had changed. It was scary to say it, or even think it, but could this be the real thing?

Dan opened the door for her and then went around to his side and climbed in. She scooted over, so she could touch him more easily, and before he turned on the engine, he squeezed her thigh. Not a big move, nothing to write home about, but it thrilled her nonetheless.

She studied him as he drove. His strong arms and hands. The way the muscles in his thighs bunched when he pushed on the clutch. His beautiful profile. Although it probably wasn't wise, she found herself wondering what it would be like to wake up next to him every day. To go to sleep, knowing he was next to her in bed.

"You're awfully quiet," he said. "Everything okay?"

"Yeah, everything's great," she said, putting her hand on his thigh. "I was just thinking."

"About?"

"You. How handsome you are. How much fun I'm having."

"Well, I can't say as how I blame you for thinking either one."

"Your modesty is blinding."

"Hey, you don't want to start things off by me being dishonest, do you?"

"Oh, no. Never."

"Well, then. I'm glad we got that straightened out."

She laughed. "And they call you grumpy. What do they know?"

He looked at her, startled. "Who calls me that?"

"Never mind."

"Come on. Out with it. Did someone really call me that?"

"No, no. I was just making conversation."

"I hope you know that I can tell when you're not telling the truth."

"You can not."

"Can so."

"How?"

"You blush. But not your embarrassed blush. You get two little pink spots way up high on your cheeks."

She reached up to feel her face, but she didn't notice any heat. "You're the one fibbing now."

"Have it your way. But be warned. I can tell."

She sniffed. "Right, Sherlock."

"You're just darn lucky we're here," he said, as he turned into the parking lot of the Blue Willow Café. "'Cause if I had you alone, I'd get the truth out of you."

"Oh, really? And how would you do that?"

He parked the truck, then turned to face her. "I'm a lawman, ma'am. A well-trained lawman."

"So you'd whip out your...gun? Is that it?"

"No, ma'am. Not with your kind. I have a different weapon for the likes of you."

"Oh, you just make me swoon when you talk like that, big boy."

"Damn, you don't make it easy, do you?"

She leaned over and gave him a quick kiss on the lips. "Nope. I make it hard." Then she scooted to her door, opened it and scrambled down. "Aren't you going to join me?"

"I need a minute," he said.

She laughed all the way into the restaurant.

DAN WAS GETTING used to the fact that everyone in the place was watching them. He didn't like it, but he didn't want to waste his time worrying about it. Let them stare. Hell, he couldn't take his eyes off Annie, either.

"I shouldn't have dessert, you know," she said.

"But I'm going to. I figure we can burn off the calories when we get home."

"Great idea," he said. "Order something real fattening."

She studied her menu, and he kept right on studying her. She was what he wanted for dessert. And for breakfast tomorrow morning, too. Whatever spell she'd cast on him was working. All his good sense seemed to have vanished, replaced by a need that only she could satisfy. Just thinking about what they were going to do back at the apartment, he could feel his body tighten.

The trouble was, every time he looked over to see Jessie Higgins sitting with Margaret Albright, he felt guilty. Their dolls were still missing, and he knew they considered Annie the culprit. Of course she wasn't, but he was spending so much time with her that solving the case had been about the last thing on his mind.

Frankly, he was stymied. He hadn't a clue. He'd put out the word at all the local markets and gas stations to notify the department of anyone new in town. He'd even gone to the lone motel and checked every person registered. Nothing looked very promising. All he knew was that he'd better figure something out by Monday.

"Dan? Order the Death-by-Chocolate for me, would you? I'll be back in a few minutes."

"Sure," he said. He watched her walk toward the rest rooms, then let his gaze wander to the other diners. Sure enough, every eye was either on him or Annie. Mostly on Annie.

"Want some dessert, Dan?"

He hadn't heard the waitress come up to the table. "The lady will have that chocolate cake, and we'll both have coffee."

"Nothing for you? We've got some nice peach pie."

He shook his head. This town was definitely too small. Everyone here knew too much about him.

Since the ordering was taken care of, he decided he'd use the facilities, too. He got up and headed back to the john, making sure not to look at Jessie and Margaret as he did so.

It didn't help. Just as he put his hand on the bathroom door, he felt a tap on his shoulder.

"Sheriff?"

He turned. The two older women were looking at him with great big sad eyes. "What can I do for you, Jessie?"

"Have you found our girls yet?"

He shook his head. "Sorry. Not yet. But the whole department is on the case."

"Is that why you're out here, dining with the prime suspect?"

"Now, come on, Margaret. There's no proof that Annie's done anything wrong."

"You said yourself that she couldn't account for her whereabouts when each of the dolls disappeared."

"That doesn't mean—"

"I just think it's smart that you're sticking so close to her. Very smart. Then, when she makes a mistake, you'll be right there to catch her."

Dan gave up. He didn't see the point in arguing with them anymore. They were going to think whatever they wanted. "You'll be the first to know if I catch her with a Barbie, okay, Margaret?"

"That's fine. Thank you, Sheriff."

The two ladies left, and Dan pushed into the peace and quiet of the bathroom.

ANNIE HAD TO LEAN up against the wall, afraid her legs weren't going to support her. She'd heard every word, and now she understood why Dan was being so attentive. Despite his denial, he *did* consider her a suspect. They all did.

How stupid was she? She'd figured everyone in the restaurant was staring because she was so happy she was glowing. Or at the very least, they'd all noticed that Dan wasn't being such a grump anymore. But now she realized they were all staring because they thought she was stealing their Barbies, and that Dan might make an arrest at any second.

She pushed open the swinging door, and headed back for the table. Without thinking twice, she got her purse from the chair, dropped a few bills on the table, and walked out. There was no way she was going to sit with him, or ride with him, or even talk with him. He'd used her in the most horrible way imaginable. And she'd let him.

More than that. She'd asked him to.

12

DAN DIDN'T REALIZE she'd gone until he saw the money on the table. At first, he just thought all the staring had made her uncomfortable, but then he got it. How could he have been so stupid? The ladies'-room door had been shut, but that didn't mean a whole lot. She must have heard his conversation with Margaret and Jessie. Scrambling to recall every word he'd said, he remembered that he'd implied she could be guilty, just to assuage the older women. Damn it.

He pulled out his wallet and left some more money just as the waitress was coming back with Annie's cake. He headed for the door.

"Hey, don't you want this?" the waitress called out.

"Keep it." Dan got to the parking lot and jogged to his truck. Annie had to be walking straight down Main. He'd catch her and explain the whole thing.

He fumbled with the keys a moment, then he was inside and on his way. He went slowly, not sure how far she would have gotten. His predicament gnawed at him even as he searched the street. The hard fact was, despite his absolute conviction that Annie was innocent, she was technically still a suspect. There was too much publicity about the case for him to simply ignore that. The women in this town all believed that Annie was the guilty party, and until he had the real thief, they would expect him to keep after her. There wasn't one woman in Harlen that would forgive him if they knew he'd actually spent the night with her, and that it had nothing to do with Barbie.

His mistake seemed quite obvious now. He should have waited until this whole mess was cleared up before he touched her. But he didn't think too clearly when he was around Annie. She stripped him of his logic, along with his clothes.

Was that her? Going into the bookstore? He sped up a bit, but then he saw that the woman was too big to be Annie. Slowing down, he continued his search, his gaze moving from one side of the street to the other as if he were at a tennis match.

What was he going to say to her when he did find her? She was going to ask for an explanation. Even if he did tell her he was convinced of her innocence, he was still going to have to explain that she wasn't in the clear. That was not going to be easy. Annie didn't know him well enough to trust him on this. She'd still wonder.

Come to think of it, he didn't know Annie that well, either. His gut told him that she wasn't the Barbie thief, and he stood by that, but if he was honest with himself, he'd have to admit that everything was happening too fast. Hadn't he made himself a promise? Hadn't he learned that his choice in women was flat-out lousy?

Was this Melissa all over again? Instead of a woman who used him as a way station on her way up the social ladder, was he now with a woman who was using him on her quest to make a tidy sum on stolen Barbies? Could his judgment be that faulty?

He didn't think so. But he hadn't believed Melissa was going to leave him until he'd been handed the divorce papers. Everyone had tried to tell him. He'd been so damn sure. Positive. The same kind of positive he was about Annie.

He slapped the wheel and cursed.

Maybe the very best thing was to let Annie be mad at him. To keep his mouth shut, go to work tomorrow and step up the investigation. Once he caught the real thief, then he could go back and see if this thing with Annie was real. If his feelings for her had changed. If he still needed her as much as he needed to breathe.

The hard part was going to be knowing she was right next door. Knowing he could walk those few steps and be in her arms, instead of his empty bed. Worse, knowing she thought he had been with her just to catch a thief.

No. He couldn't let her think that. She deserved better. The least he could do was tell her that this weekend had nothing to do with the case. She'd understand that they had to cool it for a while. Until things settled down, it would be smarter for them to keep their distance.

He was almost at their street when he saw her. She was walking fast, looking straight ahead. Her blond hair swayed over her back, and his gut ached just looking at her. Pulling the car to the curb, he slowed down to her speed and rolled down the passenger window. "Annie," he called, just as he reached her side.

She didn't even turn her head.

"Annie, please, let me explain."

"There's no need. I understand perfectly."

"Come on. Get in. You don't."

She looked at him then. "Do you have a warrant for my arrest?" she asked.

"No. Of course not."

"Then please stop bothering me." She quickened her pace.

Dan pressed the gas a little more. "I know you heard me talking to Jess and Margaret, but I didn't mean it. I know you're not the thief."

"Why didn't you say that to them?"

"Because I didn't want to get into a big discussion about it. I just wanted to come back to the table with you."

"Oh, right." She reached the corner and turned, moving faster now that the apartment was in sight.

He had to wait until a car passed, and by then she'd crossed to the other side of the street. He sped up, not trying to catch her anymore, but to beat her to the building. It was a race he intended to win.

He sped into the driveway, pulled haphazardly into his parking space and was out the door practically before he got the key out of the ignition. Then he had to run toward the front of the complex. The door was just closing, and he could see her walking to the stairs as he yanked it open again and ran after her. "Annie, damn it, wait."

"Go to hell."

"Just listen. Two minutes. That's all I ask."

"No. I won't. I won't believe you again."

He caught her right in front of her door. She spun on him, and he could see she'd been crying. And that she was livid.

"Annie, just hear me out. I promise, if you still hate me after that, fine. I'll leave you be."

"No. I listened to you the first time you said you believed me. And the second. Why should I listen to you this time?"

"I explained that. It's my job. I had to check you out because you were new in town."

"Check me out? Is that what you call last night? My, you run a very thorough sheriff's department. You don't leave any stone unturned, do you?"

"It wasn't like that. This weekend had nothing to do with the case."

"You know what? I can tell when you're lying, too. You know how? Your lips move." She yanked her arm out of his grasp, and turned her back.

Dan watched her struggle with her key. Watched her storm into her apartment. The sound of the door slamming shut was like a punch to the gut.

ANNIE HAD TO STOP crying. She just had to. Her first day teaching was tomorrow, and she didn't want her eyes to be swollen shut. It would kill her if anyone guessed what a fool she'd been. Bad enough they all thought she was a thief. She didn't want them to think she was a stupid thief.

"Annie?"

He was still at her door. Well, he could stay there all night as far as she was concerned. She wasn't going to listen to him. And she certainly wasn't going to believe in him.

"Annie, please, just listen to me. I know you're angry, and I don't blame you. But don't shut me out like this. Not after what we had this weekend."

She crossed the living room to the kitchen and got herself a drink of water. But before she even put it to her lips, she set the glass down.

"I'm not going away," he said.

His voice was muted, but his words, and his determination, were clear. She knew it was foolish, but she headed toward the door. Not that she was going to open it. Seeing him would undermine everything. She'd look into those dark brown eyes, and see that smile of his, and she'd go to pieces.

"Last night was incredible, Annie," he said. "I mean it. Maybe we shouldn't have done what we did, but it's too late to go back now. I wouldn't, even if I could."

She reached the door and leaned against it, putting her hand flat against the cool wood, next to her cheek. It was dangerous to stay, she knew that. But she couldn't seem to make her feet move.

"I didn't tell you," he said, his voice a little softer. "I should have, but I didn't. Because I didn't believe it. I know you're not guilty. But the thing is, I don't know who is. And there was all that publicity. It doesn't excuse things, but I want you to understand."

Annie sniffled, and let her body slide slowly down until she was sitting with her back against the door. She wrapped her arms around her knees and hugged tight. Tears, warm and slow, inched down her cheeks.

"Damn it, Annie, I'm not good at this. I swore I wasn't going to let this happen. I wasn't going to give a damn about anyone, ever again. Ah, hell. I just don't want it to end like this."

She didn't either. The pain in her chest was unbearable. How could she hurt so much about a guy she hardly knew? Could it really happen that quickly? Could she have fallen in love with him, just like that?

"Annie, I don't know if you're still there. You're probably not, but I'm gonna say this anyway. I never meant to hurt you. I haven't been this happy in a long, long time, and I know that you're the reason it's different. Whatever you think of me, which I know isn't very much, holding you was the best my life has been in two years. And Annie? I'd give anything to do it again."

She closed her eyes. The ache to open the door and let him in was so strong she had to grip her knees until her fingers turned white. What if he was telling her the truth? How could she know?

"Well, listen. I have to go take Cougar out. But I'm coming back. You hear that? I'm coming back."

She heard him. But she didn't open the door. She just let him go.

RACHEL DIDN'T ANSWER her phone. Which wasn't normally a big deal, but the machine didn't pick up, either. Annie blew her nose again, then went to her purse and got out the business card of the woman Rachel had rented her room from. She had to punch in the numbers twice. Something was wrong, she could feel it.

"Hello?"

"Carol? This is Annie Jones."

"Hi, how are you? It's been a long time."

"I know. I should have called before this, but with the move and all..."

"Of course. It's great to hear from you."

"Thanks. I was wondering if you knew where Rachel was."

"Oh, she didn't tell you?"

Annie's heart dropped to her shoes. "Tell me what?"

"She's doing a special project for Elliot Taylor. She'll be gone for about a week."

"Who's Elliot Taylor?"

"He's an attorney. Working on a very big case. Drug dealers or something. He needed an assistant."

Annie sat down on her bed, and tried to keep calm. "Carol, do you know him? Personally, I mean?"

"Well, no, I've never met him myself. I've heard of him, though."

"Are you sure this is on the level?"

The pause that followed made Annie more nervous than ever. "Well, I think so. But now that you mention it..."

"What?"

"Someone from the office called to ask if Rachel was coming in early Monday. It was one of the secretaries. I just assumed she didn't know about the project."

"Oh, no."

"Annie, what's wrong?"

Annie didn't want to tell Carol that Rachel had done this before. Run off with some man, told a web of lies to cover her tracks. Maybe this time, she really did have a special project. She'd known how important this job was. She'd sounded happy the last time they spoke. "Probably nothing. But could you do me a favor?"

"Sure."

"Call Greg tomorrow and find out the details. And Rachel's phone number."

"Of course, Annie. I'm sure everything's fine."

"Me, too. Thanks, Carol."

"Take care."

Annie hung up the phone and closed her eyes. She couldn't remember a time when she'd felt worse. When in hell would she learn that people don't do what they say? That they disappoint and disappear and break your heart without a backward glance? She'd needed Rachel tonight. For once. But now, instead of getting the reassurance she needed, she had to worry about her little sister again.

God, what a mess her life was in. She'd hardly slept at all last night, and today, she'd barely functioned. She hadn't eaten, except for a few peaches and some tea. Taking a shower had been awful, because all she could do was think about Dan and how she'd let herself believe.

She'd waited for him all day, of course. Heard his door open and close. For a moment, she'd thought he was at her door, but that had probably been wishful thinking. Even if he did come by, she shouldn't let him in. She knew that. But just because she knew it didn't mean she had the strength to carry it through.

The truth was, she wanted him. His strong arms. His kind eyes. She wanted to lean on him. To have him calm her fears. She tried to remember that he was only with her because he suspected her of stealing, but the longer the day went on, the harder it was to hold on to that truth.

It had felt so right. That was the problem. It had felt better than she'd ever dared hope. Could she be that wrong?

She sighed and pulled herself up. Her choices didn't seem very appealing. She could worry about Rachel or obsess about Dan. Great. It was going to be a long night.

THE KNOCK on the door startled her and she almost dropped her plate of warmed-up lasagna. Her reaction was swift. The tightness in her stomach, the trembling she felt wash through her. It was Dan. It had to be Dan.

The whole way to the living room, she told herself she wasn't going to let him in. She couldn't. He'd betrayed her, he'd told those women that he suspected her of stealing.

"Annie? You there?"

Just the tone of his voice made her cringe. He sounded lost, alone, like he needed her. But how could she believe him? How could she believe anything, ever again?

"Cougar says hey."

She went up to the door and reached for the knob. But she just held it, knowing that to turn it might be the biggest mistake of her life.

"Honey, I'm so sorry. I..."

She turned the knob slowly. Pulled the door open. Then he was in front of her. She looked up into his eyes, and the tears came.

His arms went around her and she buried her face in his chest. She felt his hand petting her hair in long slow strokes, heard his soft, "Shhh, baby. It's okay."

"Rachel's gone," she said, mumbling into his damp shirt.

"What? I didn't understand you."

She lifted her head. "Rachel's gone. And you think I'm a thief. And everything is just awful."

He took his hands and cupped her cheeks, holding her gaze steady. "Baby, it's okay. I promise. I don't think you're a thief. And we'll find your sister. I give you my word."

She sniffled. Oh, how she longed to believe him. How she longed to be held, and for once in her life, to let someone else do the worrying. But how could she give in?

He leaned closer. Closer. His lips touched hers. She succumbed.

13

DAN PULLED ANNIE to his chest again, hugging her as tightly as he could without hurting her. He knew he wasn't doing the smart thing. But he believed he was doing the right thing.

"Come on, honey. Let's go inside."

Annie let him shut the door and lead her to the couch. He sat on the end, and she curled up beside him. She hadn't stopped crying, although she wasn't trembling anymore.

"Now, what's this about Rachel?" he asked.

"The woman she's staying with said she went on some kind of special assignment, but I know Rachel. She's pulled this kind of thing before. She probably got bored and ran off with some man. Dan, this means she won't get her tuition for next year. I tried my best. I found her the job, I even agreed to come here, all so she'd have this chance. And she can't even stay two weeks."

"Are you sure she's run off?"

"No. Not sure."

"Well, what about giving her the benefit of the doubt?"

"Been there, done that," she said, bringing a crumpled tissue to her eyes. "I want to trust her.

Honestly. But all I seem to do is get her out of one fix after another."

"Maybe it's time for Rachel to get herself out of a fix or two."

Annie looked up at him. "She's my sister."

"I know. But you can't always be there, no matter how much you'd like to be. She's going to have to learn to depend on herself at some point."

"I'm all she has. I pretty much raised her after Mom died."

"What about your father?"

"He died sixteen years ago. My mother died nine years ago. So really, it's just been the two of us ever since I was eighteen."

"That's a lot of responsibility."

"I don't want any more responsibility. I didn't ask for it. But I can't let her throw her life away."

He brought his free hand up to her cheek. "Why don't we try to find her together? Let me do some of the worrying this time?"

She smiled. Her eyes were red, a little swollen, and she had mascara smudged underneath. But to him she was the most beautiful woman he'd ever seen. "I start teaching tomorrow."

"That's right. Why don't you come by the department at lunch?"

She sniffled. "Everyone in town will think I'm there to turn myself in."

"You let me worry about that, too. I'm gonna find out who's stealing those Barbies. I promise."

"I hope so. You know, for a minute there, I'd

actually thought about staying. Not going back to Houston. But now…"

"Really? You've thought about staying?"

"I don't know. Maybe. A little."

"But…?"

"Well, Rachel. I don't see how I can leave her. And, of course, there's the fact that no one here likes me or trusts me."

"They just don't know you. As for Rachel, I have a hunch she's going to surprise you."

"Maybe. I don't know. I don't know much of anything anymore."

"You're just tired. That's my fault. I haven't made this a very easy weekend for you, have I?

She sniffled a little and snuggled a little closer. God, he liked having her near. He didn't want to fight with Annie again. Ever.

But hearing her talk about staying… That was a whole different matter. He'd come to her knowing she was only here for the summer. That it couldn't be permanent between them. He didn't want permanent, even with someone as special as Annie. Now wasn't the time to bring that up, but at some point, he was going to have to tell her. There's no way he was going to marry anyone again. Especially not Annie. He wouldn't be able to stand it if he failed her.

"I need to go get some more tissue," Annie said, sitting up. "Do you want some coffee or something?"

He shook his head. "No, but if you do, I'll make it. It's the least I can do."

She looked at him for a long moment, then her lips curled slightly. "You're right. It is the least you can do. What I want to know is what's the most?"

He smiled. "Now don't get me started. It's a school night, and we both need to get some sleep."

Her smile faded, and something in her eyes darkened. Almost as if a light had gone out. "Of course, you're right." She stood up and went in search of her tissue.

Dan knew he'd disappointed her. She'd wanted him to stay the night. A large part of him wanted that too, but for once he was listening to his head instead of his hormones. They both needed some time to think, and Annie was exhausted. Tomorrow, when he had more of a handle on the missing Barbies, and Annie had finished her first day of school, they'd talk again. He didn't want to mislead her. And he didn't want to take advantage of her.

But he wished he hadn't been looking into her eyes.

ANNIE WIPED her eyes, cleaning up a little of her mascara. She didn't want to look so pathetic when she went to the living room. She certainly didn't want Dan to see how deeply he'd disappointed her. Of course, she had no business expecting him to stay. They didn't have a real relationship, after all. This was just a temporary fling, purely physical. That's all she'd asked for, and that's all she got, so why the hell did his rejection hurt so much?

She had no business getting involved with a man. At least not a man she liked as much as Dan. He'd told her the truth from the beginning. She was the one who wanted the ground rules changed. It wasn't fair to be angry. He'd been very nice to her, and he hadn't lied.

There was only one problem. She'd fallen for him. Big-time. How that could happen in just a few days was a mystery to her, but she knew with absolute certainty that it was true.

It wasn't as if she'd planned to. But it had happened anyway. So now what? She couldn't tell him. She couldn't act on it. She didn't even feel right thinking about it. Maybe the best thing was just to stop seeing him. He was right, deciding not to spend the night. She should be grateful. Once he was out of her apartment, out of her sight, she'd see things more rationally. She'd stop wishing for more. This ache in her heart would go away.

She picked up her compact and powdered her nose, then ran a brush through her hair. A quick practice smile in the mirror, and she was ready to say goodbye to Dan.

He wasn't on the couch. He had gone to the

kitchen, where he was putting the kettle on the stove.

"Change your mind?" she asked, pleased that her voice sounded completely normal.

"I owed you that cup of coffee," he said.

"You don't owe me anything," she said. She moved next to him and turned off the burner. "But you were right. It is a school night, and I am pretty tired."

"I didn't mean to upset you," he said.

She didn't look at him. "You didn't. I just want to go to bed."

He sighed. "Will you come by tomorrow at lunch?"

"I'll try."

He was silent for a long time. Annie finally stopped staring at her feet and met his gaze. It was a mistake. Dan looked as hurt as she felt. Well, she couldn't help that. She walked past him to the living room, heading for the door.

"Annie?"

She stopped. "Yes?"

"I want to be with you. Honestly, I do. It's just that—"

"Please don't. I understand. I agree. Tonight isn't the night."

He came over to her and put his hands on her shoulders, turning her to face him. She stared at his chest, at the little wet spot where she'd cried.

"Why won't you look at me?" he asked, his voice so gentle she almost lost it again.

"I got a wrong idea. That's all. No big deal."

"What wrong idea?"

"Nothing. It has nothing to do with you. It's my own foolishness."

"Tell me."

"No. I won't. It's not important. But there is something I want to show you."

He waited, looking at her curiously. She'd thought about this today, in all those hours when she relived every moment she'd shared with him. Opening her hall closet, she went to the top box. The one he'd spilled that first night. She brought it out and put it on the couch.

"What's this?"

She didn't answer him. Instead, she reached into the box and brought out a doll. It was no Barbie. Nothing half so fashionable. Her doll was old and ragged, with scratches and missing clumps of hair. The clothes were clean, but torn. She turned to Dan. "This is what you saw the other night. It wasn't a Barbie."

"I know that. You don't have to convince me."

"I do. I know that you want to believe I'm innocent, but I also know you have a job to do. That everyone in this town thinks of me as a thief. I didn't want you wondering. That's all."

"You've had that for a long time," he said, his voice so soft it almost had her crying.

"It was my mother's doll."

"I see."

She put the baby doll carefully back in the box. "Okay, then."

He reached over and took her arm, pulling her toward him. She knew he was going to kiss her. And when he did, she couldn't be responsible. Not for anything. Before she lost her nerve she broke away from his grasp and opened the door. "Good night."

"Why does that sound so much like goodbye?"

She blinked back a fresh batch of tears. "Please?"

"I'll go. But this isn't over. I won't let it be over." He walked to the door, looked at her one last time, then stepped into the hallway.

She couldn't shut the door fast enough.

DAN STOOD in front of her door for a long time. Things had gone wrong, but he wasn't exactly sure how or why. Only that he'd bungled what they'd had going.

For a moment there, he'd had her. Then, he'd blown it, even though he'd thought he was doing the right thing. Who could tell with women? It was as if they had a secret password that would make them perfectly happy, but that he'd only been given four of the six letters. He kept getting reasonably close, but then he'd type in the last two, and they'd shut down, barring him access.

He thought about talking to her through the door again. That had worked. But he doubted it would this time. That was another thing. He was never sure whether to repeat something good. Sometimes it worked like a charm. Other times, he got that look.

He'd been right all along. He'd be better off not even trying. Cougar was enough company for anyone. Okay, except for that one thing. But as he'd reckoned before, he'd best take care of that out of town.

Shaking his head, he went back to his apartment. But even there he was in for disappointment. Cougar, who was curled up on the couch, barely lifted his head in greeting, then went back to sleep.

Dan just sighed.

MORNING CAME, and Dan was anxious to get to work. He'd not had the good night's sleep he needed. He kept listening for her. By the sound of it, she hadn't slept well either. At one point, sometime after midnight, he'd heard her leave the apartment. It made him nervous, so he got dressed and went to look for her. But she had just taken out some trash. Through the small crack of his open door, he'd seen her return with a white plastic bin.

After that, he'd heard water running for a long time. A bath, he'd guess. Then nothing till morning.

He doubted she was going to leave this early, and he didn't want to wake her, but once he was ready for work, standing outside her door in the hallway, he had to struggle not to knock. Maybe he should write her a note. What would he say? With a shrug, he decided to let it be.

He turned away, and stepped on something on the carpet. Looking down, he couldn't quite make it out, so he bent and picked it up. His chest clenched. "Oh, damn," he whispered. It was a tiny shoe. The kind that fitted a Barbie doll.

ANNIE LOOKED at the entrance to the Y, at all the people walking in and out. The building was equipped with a full gym, and adult classes were being offered along with the children's art workshops for which she was responsible. It seemed to her it was the busiest place in Harlen. Before she'd realized the whole town thought she was a thief, that had been a plus. A great way to meet neighbors, and hopefully, new friends. Now, she just hoped they wouldn't stone her in public.

But she had a job to do, and the heck with them if they thought she wasn't going to do it.

She transferred her bag of supplies to her other arm, straightened her shoulders and walked on.

Pushing the door open, she stepped inside, enjoying the rush of cool air that met her. Her classroom was to the right, but the administrative offices were to the left, and she debated for a moment before deciding just to get on with it. She'd only have a half hour before her kids started to arrive, and she wanted to be ready.

Several people looked at her as she made her

way down the long corridor. She didn't blink. Or even let herself get flustered. Letting them get to her would be tantamount to admitting she'd done something wrong, which she hadn't.

Room 12B was hers, and she opened the door gingerly, expecting who knew what to greet her. A mob of angry Barbie owners? Instead, she saw a wide open space filled with pint-sized easels, a big blackboard on one end, and lots of hooks for aprons on the other. Lining the far wall were boxes of materials like clay and crayons. Plenty of light came in from the big windows, and the moment she set foot inside the room she felt better.

The half hour to get ready was barely enough. One little girl named Peggy, Annie discovered after a moment of questioning, always came in ten minutes early and therefore got to help fill paper cups with water.

By ten, the big room didn't look so big anymore, once all her eighteen charges had arrived. They each had an apron on, and the very first project of the day was to write name tags. She drew an example on the wall using her own name. Then she walked around, helping with the crucial decision of what color to choose.

The kids seemed nice, and they were eager, which was all to her advantage. At least here she was on sure footing. The name tags were coming out wonderfully. It was if she could breathe for the first time since last night.

"Miss Jones?"

She identified the girl who'd called out to her by the waving arm. "Yes, Debbi?"

"If I bring my Barbie here, will you steal it?"

Annie's breath left her once again. She felt herself flush, and she had to still the urge to simply run away. "No, Debbi. Your Barbie will be perfectly safe here."

"Yeah, that's what I thought. My mom said she thought you might be taking the Barbies but I said you were a teacher, and they're not allowed to steal."

"That was very nice of you, Debbi. Now, how is that name tag coming along?"

She managed to say the right words, to laugh when one of the kids said something amusing, to look concerned when the painting didn't go according to plan. But all she could think about was her pretty dreams and how they had all turned to dust.

LUNCHTIME. Annie stood in front of the sheriff's office, looking up at the second floor window where she imagined Dan was sitting.

There was only one reason she was here, and that was because of Rachel. She'd called Carol just fifteen minutes before, and had gone from mildly worried to pretty panicked.

Elliot Taylor was, in fact, an attorney, but according to Carol, there was something fishy about him. No one at the office seemed to know anything about the special project Rachel was supposedly helping with, and the two people who would be the most likely to have real information were in Austin for three days. Three days! There was no way Annie could wait that long to find out if Rachel was in trouble.

So she had to go to Dan, and ask for his help. Just yesterday, she would have thanked her lucky stars that Dan was her neighbor and the first person she'd gotten to know in Harlen. Now she cursed her bad luck.

But there was no time to waste. She headed across the street and up the stairs. Once inside, she got to the elevator, and, because the universe had a wonderful sense of humor, one of the women from the restaurant last night climbed in next to her. Annie didn't recall her name, but she wore a name badge. Surreptitiously glancing when the woman wasn't outright staring at her, Annie saw that she was Jessie.

"Morning," Annie said, right that second deciding she wasn't going to play this game.

Jessie turned to her, eyes wide. "Morning."

"Yes, it's me. The one who everyone thinks is a Barbie thief."

Jessie coughed, then pressed the second-floor button about five times. "I don't... You couldn't... Here we are!"

The door barely opened enough for the woman to squeeze out and she was gone. Annie watched her rush down the hall, her rubber-soled shoes squeaking a feverish tempo.

Actually, Annie didn't care. She'd taken the offensive, and that was what was important. Infinitely encouraged, she headed for Dan's office. She didn't blush once, no matter who stared at her or what they whispered to each other.

Seeing Dan made her hesitate, but not for long. She just marched right up to him. When he saw her, he broke out into a Texas-size grin. Her heart fairly leapt out of her chest at the sight. But the closer she got, the more the smile faded, until, when she was squarely in front of him, there wasn't even a memory left.

Instead, his face was filled with worry. She didn't want to know why.

"I didn't think you were going to come," he said, touching her arm so briefly she might have imagined it.

"It's Rachel."

"Bad news?"

She nodded. "I know it's an imposition, but I really do need your help. I'm awfully worried she's running with someone who could hurt her."

"No need to ask twice. Let's head over to my desk so I can take down the particulars."

This time, his touch was real and steady. Right on the center of her back. She wanted to jerk away, to make him promise never to touch her again, especially when his hands were so large and warm and made her think of all the things that could have been. But she didn't. She just walked.

He was the one to stop short. Right inside his office, she felt him freeze beside her. Looking up, she saw his gaze was riveted to his desk. She stopped breathing as she followed his stare.

At first she didn't recognize it. It was so small. But then the shape made sense. A little plastic high heel. A Barbie accessory if she'd ever seen one. Something was under it. A note card.

She stepped forward, feeling Dan grab at her, but he was too late. She saw the card. Read the note. "Evidence found outside Annie Jones's apartment, 7:14 a.m."

She turned slowly to face him. "We can go back to my place right now, and you can search every cupboard and shelf. But you'd better bring a female officer with you. I wouldn't want your investigation compromised any more than it already has been."

14

THE LIGHT CLICKED on with such intensity that Dan was blinded for a moment. He put his hand in front of his eyes and walked toward the source. "What the hell?"

"Sheriff, are you going to make an arrest?"

When Dan could see again, there was a bulbous microphone in his face held by a reporter from a Houston television station. She was dressed in gray, and her hair was dark, and in some other circumstance he might have found her attractive. But right now it was all he could do not to shove her bodily out of his office.

"No, I'm not going to make an arrest. You're not allowed in my office without invitation— Hey, get that camera off of her unless you're looking for a lawsuit, buddy."

The cameraman swung away from Annie and focused on him again. The reporter was still there, too.

"Did you hear me?"

"Isn't it true you've found material evidence in the Barbie-snatching case?"

"I have, yes, but it's not enough evidence to

make an arrest. If you haven't noticed, there are millions of Barbies out there."

"But this material evidence was at the home of a chief suspect, isn't that right?"

"No, it is not right. Would you please step outside? I'll be happy to make a statement to all of you at 3:00 p.m., but I won't say any more right now."

"But, Sheriff—"

"Out!"

The woman made a slicing motion at her throat and the horrible camera light went out. The reporter turned to her associate. "Did you get her?"

He nodded as he swung the camera down to his side. "And the evidence."

"If you use that, I'll personally sue your ass off," Dan said, advancing on the cameraman. "And I'll be more than happy to lock the door once I put you behind bars."

"Hey, you ever heard of freedom of the press?" the man said, backing away. He wasn't a very big guy.

"Yes, I have. But I've also heard of due process. We have a library down the street. Why don't you look it up?"

The reporter and her buddy stepped outside his office, and Dan slammed the door in their faces. Then he turned to Annie. "You okay? I'm sorry about that."

"Sorry?" Annie said as she leaned against his desk. She looked pale and shaky, and for a moment he thought she might faint. Instead, she pulled herself together. She stood up straight and gave him a defiant look. "I'm just sorry I ever came to Harlen. This isn't a nice town. Matter of fact, it pretty much sucks."

"Annie, it's just that this weird story has gotten out of hand. I know this town. Or at least I thought I did. The folks are like most folks, nothing out of the ordinary. But something like this, with the reporters and all. It's just human nature to speculate."

"Speculating is one thing. Calling me a thief on the network news is something else again."

"I'll make sure they don't use that footage."

"And what if they follow me? I'm teaching today, Dan. Teaching little kids. One of whom has already asked if I was the lady who stole Barbies."

Dan cursed. "All I can tell you is I'm trying like hell to find out who's really stealing these dolls. The sooner I catch the real thief, the sooner you can have your life back."

"Do you have any leads? Other than the shoe you found at my place?"

He shook his head, wishing that he could answer her another way.

"It was planted there, you know. Someone's trying to make me look guilty."

"I realize that."

"Do you?"

He took two steps toward her, but she backed

away so fast he could see she didn't want to be touched. And that's all he wanted to do. Take her in his arms and tell her everything was going to be all right. That she could count on him. That he'd take care of her. But he couldn't tell her any of those things, because he was still without another suspect. "I don't believe you're stealing Barbies, Annie. I told you that before."

She turned and picked up the evidence card. "But you still wrote this?"

He looked down. "I can't destroy evidence, Annie. It could lead us to the real thief."

"I understand completely," she said, putting the card back. "You have your job to do."

"That's true. But don't forget, I'm on your side."

"Until the evidence mounts up and the town pressures you to do something about it."

"That's not fair."

"But it's accurate."

He looked up at her again, and wanted to tell her that she was wrong. But she wouldn't believe him. He didn't blame her. All he could do at this point was show her. And catch that damn thief.

"I'd still like you to help me with Rachel, if that's not breaking some rule."

He hurried behind his desk, and reached for a missing person's report. Pointing to the chair across from him, he said, "Sit, please."

She did. And she gave him the information about her sister in a cool, logical manner. All the while he was writing, he remembered their weekend. Remembered holding her in his arms. Making love to her until they both had to collapse from sheer exhaustion. Watching her sleep. Feeling, for the first time in his life, that he had found the one woman who could really make him happy.

Knowing that she never wanted to see him again.

ANNIE LEFT the sheriff's department in something of a daze. She could hardly believe all that had happened to her. Not the least of which was the cadre of reporters waiting to ambush her a few steps from the door.

Walking as quickly as she could, she stared straight ahead and didn't acknowledge the barrage of questions coming at her from all sides. Lights flashed in her eyes, but she just kept on walking. The last thing she wanted to do was engage any of these horrible people in conversation. She didn't need to deny any wrongdoing. As far as she was concerned, they were the thieves, stealing her happiness away from her in huge chunks.

They didn't give up until she was across the street, and almost inside the Y. She thought she saw Kirstie Collins standing on the sidelines, but she couldn't be sure, and she wasn't going to dawdle to find out.

Once she got inside, she slowed her pace. As

she headed to what was once her dream job, she made up her mind. She would leave Harlen, and the job, and Dan, and go back home.

Why linger when all chances of a new life here had been snatched away just as cleanly as the missing Barbies? It wasn't so bad, was it? She liked her apartment in Houston. She liked her job, even though it didn't fulfill her the way she'd always hoped it would. Then she thought about Dan, and she had to stop kidding herself. Leaving would be hell. Because she would never forget him.

She hated whoever was stealing the Barbies. Hated them with a passion she barely recognized. They'd stolen Dan from her, and that was one loss she wasn't prepared to take. He'd been with her so briefly, yet the promise of what they could have had together was crystal-clear in her mind.

She knew, without a doubt, that Dan was *the one*. The one she'd waited all her life for. The one she wanted to spend the rest of her days with. She'd fallen in love, just like that. She had a feeling it would take a whole lot longer to fall out of love. Maybe forever.

The kids were all in the classroom when she walked in. The seven- and eight-year-olds looked so darling in their little aprons, she had to smile.

Would she ever have a child of her own? It was so easy to imagine what Dan's child would look like. What their child could be. And that, too, had been ripped away like a page from a notebook.

"Everybody have a good lunch?" she asked.

A chorus of *yesses* met her as she went to put on her own apron. "Now, everyone carefully touch your name tag with one finger," she said. "Make sure it's dry, and then one at a time come up here and I'll pin it on your apron. That's going to be your name tag for the rest of the summer, so don't play with it."

She went back to the front of the class and brought out the box of safety pins. Soon a line formed, and each of the kids, one by one, proudly handed over their first piece of art.

"This is wonderful, Kevin!" she said as she pinned the first tag on. Kevin rewarded her with a brilliant smile, and she had to swallow hard not to tear up. Damn it, she'd come so close. The pull to be with these kids, to watch as they learned that they had the power to create pretty things, was overwhelming. But how could she stay? Even they thought she was the thief, and it would only get worse as they started seeing her picture on television.

As soon as the class was over, she would go and tender her resignation. Then she'd go home and call the movers, and start packing. That decided, she renewed her enthusiasm with the kids, wanting them to know, somehow, that she believed in each and every one of them.

DAN RAN a quick hand through his hair as he walked downstairs to meet the press. He was angry, and that wasn't good. He'd have to stay calm if he wanted to handle this situation well. But he hated these press people, with their intrusions and assumptions, and he wanted them to leave and never come back.

Barbies. All because of Barbies. Who would have thought such an innocent little doll could cause all this havoc?

He left the stairwell and was met by the crowd of vultures. The questions started, all at once, so he could barely make anything out.

Behind the CNN cameraman, he caught sight of his sister. She waved frantically for his attention—no, for the attention of the press.

"Hello! Excuse me. Please, everyone. This way!"

One or two of the reporters heard her and turned, then the rest of them, like lemmings, followed suit. He was now at the back of the throng and Kirstie had center stage.

"Thank you. My name is Kirstie Collins and I broke the original story on the Barbie thefts."

She really had their attention now. Lights focused on her face, and microphones pushed in to get every word.

"I'm afraid this has gotten completely out of hand. There really is no story. The Barbies are safe, every one of them, and they'll all be returned to their rightful owners soon."

"Who took them?"

"Did you find them in Annie Jones's apartment?"

"Where are they now?"

"How much were they worth?"

Kirstie lifted her arms for quiet, but it didn't help much. "I'll be releasing a statement in the next couple of days. That's all. Just go back home. The story is over."

"Wait a minute," the Houston reporter said. "What the hell's going on here? Are you just trying to get rid of us so you'll have the exclusive?"

"No, that's not it at all. I'm just trying to explain—"

The Houston reporter turned her back on Kirstie and headed toward Dan. "You said you'd have a statement for us. We saw that you had evidence that Annie Jones from Houston was connected to the missing Barbies. Are you saying now that the Barbies were found in her possession?"

Dan looked over at Kirstie, wondering what she was doing. Trying to protect him? To protect Annie? If she'd really found the Barbies, she would have come to him. Now, he couldn't ask her, not with this horde of reporters surrounding them. "No, I'm not saying that. The investigation is still underway. No new leads have turned up. That's all."

"Isn't Kirstie Collins your sister?"

"What are you two trying to pull?"

He elbowed his way through the crowd until

he was right next to Kirstie. He bent down next to her so he could whisper in her ear. "What *are* you trying to pull?"

"I can't explain now. But I will. Soon. Just don't do anything rash."

"Rash? What the hell are you talking about, Kirstie?"

"Just trust me. I've got to go. I'll talk to you later."

Dan stood, flabbergasted, as he watched his sister make a break for it, leaving him to deal with the mob on his own. Something very fishy was going on and he needed time to think it through. There was one thing he could do now, though.

He turned back to the reporters. "I'm calling a town meeting tonight at the county courthouse. You're all welcome to attend, if you behave yourselves. If anything out of line happens, the doors will be bolted."

"Are you going to announce an arrest tonight, Sheriff?"

"You'll see tonight. That's all." He left them then, keeping his pace quick but steady. Their questions bounced off his back like pebbles. Especially one…

"Are you going to arrest Annie Jones?"

ANNIE HEARD about the town meeting long before she had a chance to resign. One of the mothers broke the news to her. Debbi's mother, to be exact.

Annie was standing by the sink, washing paint-brushes, checking from time to time to make sure her charges were hanging up aprons in an orderly fashion, when she sensed someone standing next to her. She turned, a bit afraid it was going to be a reporter, but then saw it was a woman in her thirties holding Debbi's hand.

"I'm Mrs. Franklin," she said, eyeing Annie like a side of beef at the market. "I like the name tag."

Annie picked up a few paper towels to dry her hands. "Thank you. Debbi is quite talented."

"She's always loved to draw. That's why we signed her up for this class."

"Well, she's a very welcome student."

"So," Mrs. Franklin said, leaning in and lowering her voice. "Some excitement about tonight, eh?"

Annie got a bad feeling. Right in the pit of her stomach. "Pardon?"

"You know. The town meeting. It's all anyone can talk about."

"I'm sorry, I don't know what you mean."

Mrs. Franklin's eyes widened. "You haven't heard?"

"Obviously not."

"Sheriff Collins has called a town meeting for tonight. He's going to make a statement about..." she waggled her perfectly shaped eyebrows "...you know."

"I'm afraid I don't." Annie did, of course. She

just couldn't bring herself to admit it to this strange woman.

"The Barbies." She just mouthed the words as if saying them aloud would taint her.

"Ah, yes."

"I'm on your side, hon. Debbi says you were real nice to her today."

"Well, thank you. I'm sorry, I have to make sure everyone gets ready to leave."

"I'll see you tonight then."

"I wouldn't miss it for the world."

Mrs. Franklin smiled, then pulled her daughter after her through the maze of easels and out the door.

Annie felt her shoulders droop, and for the life of her she couldn't move. Her legs felt like lead and her head hurt. All she wanted to do was crawl under her covers and never come out again. But then the rest of the parents started traipsing in, and she could tell each one of them was sizing her up, reaching their own conclusion based on... What? Her hair? How well little Johnny painted his name? It was all so crazy. All so sad and crazy.

Finally, she was alone. She pulled a piece of paper from her bag and wrote out her resignation. It took all her energy to walk down the corridor to the administrative office. The program director who'd hired her wasn't in, and she ended up handing her note to a secretary who wanted to know if she'd heard about the town meeting, and if she didn't, it was going to be held at the County

Courthouse at seven-thirty. But Annie should probably get there at seven. Considering.

Annie just nodded. This time, she couldn't even muster a smile.

The walk home was awful, and facing the job of packing up all her belongings was worse. She began in the kitchen. She cried her way through three boxes before she just had to give up.

"ANNIE?" Dan had been knocking for several minutes. He should probably give up, but he couldn't. "Annie, please open up. I have information about Rachel."

He waited again, and just before he figured he'd pack it in, the door opened. Annie let him in, but she didn't look at him. He could tell she'd been crying. Without even thinking, he reached out for her, scooping her up in his arms.

She didn't fight. Her head came to rest on his chest and she wrapped her arms around his waist.

"Honey, I'm so sorry about this," he said, moving so he could rub his chin gently on her hair. "I'm going to fix it. I swear. Tonight. I'm going to make sure no one hurts you, ever again."

"You don't have to worry," she said, moving her right hand so she could wipe her tears. "I'm leaving. I don't want to stay here anymore."

"Leaving?" He pulled back so he could look at her. She was obviously miserable and, damn it, he wanted to fix it. "Please, don't. Not yet. Wait until tonight. I swear everything will get better."

"How can it? Unless you've found out who the real thief is."

He shook his head. "Nope. Although I think Kirstie might be on to something. I've tried calling her, but she's not home."

Annie let go of him and walked over to the couch. She curled her legs under her and sat on the very edge. Looking very young, she dabbed her eyes with a crumpled piece of tissue. "You said you had some information about Rachel?"

"Yeah, and it's not bad." He went over and sat next to her on the couch, wanting very much to change her position so he could hold her again. "The lawyer she's evidently working with is pretty well-known. He's defended a lot of big cases in Texas. His reputation is that he's ruthless, thorough, but ethical."

"But why would he take Rachel away from the firm?"

"I found out about that, too. Evidently, they're holed up somewhere, working to get ready for a big case. He's done this before. Taken an assistant."

"A young, beautiful assistant?"

Dan shrugged. "I couldn't get that much information."

"So where are they staying?"

"I don't know. Yet. But we'll hear. I'm sure

she's fine, Annie. I would have felt it if something was wrong."

"Felt it?"

"I've got pretty good instincts about these things." He smiled.

"Thank you," she said. "I mean it. I know you didn't have to do this for me."

"Didn't have to?" He put his hand on her shoulder, needing much more contact. "I wanted to."

She looked at her hands for a moment. "I want you to search the apartment."

"What?"

"I said, I want you to search the apartment. Everywhere. I want you to see with your own eyes that I don't have any Barbies here."

He reached over and lifted her chin with his finger. "I don't need to."

"Yes, you do. You're the sheriff, Dan. You have to be certain."

"I am."

"If you were certain, you wouldn't have put my name on that card."

"Now, come on. I had to put down where I found it. I think someone put it there so I would find it. It's evidence."

"But that reporter took my picture."

"I'll take care of the media tonight. Just let me handle it, okay?"

Slowly, after a long silent time, she nodded. "I hate this," she whispered. "I thought I'd actually found a place I could live. Where I could be happy. It's too late now."

"No, it's not. I swear it's not."

"Even if you do find out the truth, people aren't going to change their minds so quickly. I study sociology, remember? I know some things about human nature."

"All they have to do is get to know you. They'll see right away that you're a remarkable woman."

She met his gaze. "Is that what you think?"

He nodded. "Yes, I do. I admire how you've handled yourself through this. It's been rough, and you've been a real trooper."

"Not today I haven't. I quit at the Y."

"You can unquit tomorrow."

"I don't know."

He caressed the side of her face, once more amazed at the softness, the vulnerability of her. "I don't want you to go."

"Why not? I'd be leaving at the end of the summer, anyway."

"A lot can happen in a summer."

Annie uncurled her legs and moved over so that her body and his touched from shoulder to knee. She took both his hands in hers and looked up at him earnestly. "A lot has happened in a weekend. Dan, I..."

He knew what she was going to say, and he wished she wouldn't. He didn't know how he was going to respond. Annie was a remarkable woman, and he liked her more than he would ever have guessed. But was it love? Was she the one he was going to break all the rules for? Damn it, he wasn't sure. And that was the last thing Annie needed to hear.

"I—"

He leaned over and took the words from her lips with a kiss.

15

ANNIE LET HIM kiss her silent. The words themselves hadn't mattered. His reaction had. She knew now for certain that Dan didn't love her. He hadn't fallen like she had. It was too much to expect, after all.

She pulled back, afraid her tears would start again. She didn't want him to see her disappointment. It wasn't his fault. They'd been together such a short time. How could she possibly expect him to feel the way she did? Just because she'd gone over the edge, it didn't mean he had to follow.

"You okay?" he whispered.

"Yeah, I'm fine." She stood up, and forced a smile. "Can I get you something?"

"No. I have to get over to the courthouse. Come with me?"

"I don't want to go. I don't think I can handle it."

"It's up to you, but I'd like it if you came. It'll be rough at first, but I guarantee, by the end of the night, everything will be squared away."

She wanted to believe him. But facing those reporters...the stares, the accusations. No, she was too shaky. Especially now that she knew Dan's feelings. What she needed was some time, time to think things through and make some decisions. "I'll see," she said.

He stood up and she walked him to the door. Once it was open, though, he turned back to her. "Annie…" he said, then she was in his arms. He kissed her and this time it wasn't to silence her. There was an urgency to his lips. His arms held her almost too tightly.

A flash of light jerked her out of his embrace. A reporter stood in the hallway, ready to take another picture. Dan turned on him furiously. "Give me that camera."

"No way." The reporter turned and ran down the hall, with Dan chasing him full speed.

Annie stared after them, still too stunned to speak. Couldn't anything go right for them? Couldn't they just get one break?

She hated to think what this picture could mean. Once it was out there, would anyone believe Dan when he said she was innocent? It was bad enough so many people had seen them eating together. But kissing? In her apartment?

It was the last straw. She had no more energy to fight. Closing the door, she looked around her apartment. She couldn't pack. Not tonight. All she needed tonight was to throw a few things into a suitcase and get into her car. She'd deal with the rest of it later.

She was going home.

DAN GAVE UP chasing the bastard halfway to Main Street. He couldn't take the camera anyway or he'd face charges. Damn it, things just went from bad to worse.

He hurried back to the apartment and went to Annie's door. He knocked for a long time before she opened it. She didn't step aside to let him in, though.

"I didn't get the camera," he said.

"Okay."

"But don't worry. It'll still be all right."

"I'm not worried. Thank you for trying."

"Will you come with me?"

She shook her head. "No, I'm sorry. I appreciate all you're trying to do, but I just don't have the energy. I can't face them."

He wasn't going to press the point. Annie'd been through enough. "I'll come by after, okay?"

She gave him a weak smile. "Sure."

The door closed quietly. Somehow, Dan knew it was closed for good.

HE TRIED CALLING Kirstie three more times before he left. Each time, he got her answering machine. Finally, he couldn't wait any longer. He had to go.

By the time he reached the courthouse, the parking lot was almost full. There were television vans lined up on the east walkway, their huge antennae making the vehicles look like they were from outer space.

People were coming in groups, in pairs, and

singly. The women were dressed as if they were going to church, in summer dresses and high-heeled sandals. The men looked less enthusiastic, but they too were wearing their Sunday best.

Dan felt like he was watching the Romans enter the arena. That in the middle of the meeting he would hear a huge cry, and the townspeople of Harlen, Texas, would jump to their feet and cry out for the lions to be let loose.

He'd always loved this town. But not tonight. Tonight he just felt ashamed. For all of them. Mostly, for himself. He'd messed up several times in his life, but he couldn't remember ever hurting someone so innocent before. He should have stopped this nonsense days ago. Before the media had turned it into a circus. Before Annie looked at him so hopelessly.

No one spoke to him as he climbed the steps. They all drifted sideways, giving him a wide berth. He wasn't sure why. Maybe because they saw his anger. His sadness. But he doubted it. To them he was a player in tonight's drama. One of the stars.

Inside, the room was filling up quickly. Kirstie was on stage already, as was his brother Reese. It was an awfully long walk up to that stage.

When he got there, a hush settled over the crowd. Even the newspeople settled down. Kirstie approached the microphone before he could reach it.

"I have something to say," she said.

Dan walked up to her and took the mike out of her hand. "Later, Kirstie. It's my turn."

"But, Dan. You don't understand."

"I do understand. Now go on. Sit down."

Kirstie looked at Reese. He shrugged. Dan turned to the audience. "I know why you're all here tonight. You're all expecting me to make an arrest. To tell you that Annie Jones is the person who's been stealing the Barbie dolls. Well, that's—" Dan stopped. He tried to see through the crowd standing at the back. Yes, it was her. Annie. She was here.

"Sheriff Collins?"

His attention was drawn to a man, a reporter from CNN, standing to the side of the stage.

"Is it true Annie Jones came to Harlen in response to your personal ad in *Texas Men* magazine?"

"What?"

"This ad?" The man held up a magazine, and although he was standing pretty far away, Dan recognized himself on the page.

"What is that?"

"It's a want ad. For a wife."

"I don't know what kind of a joke this is, but it's not funny. I never put an ad in any magazine."

"So you weren't looking for a wife?"

"No, I most certainly was not." Dan froze, realizing what he just said. His eyes searched the back of the room for Annie. She had the door open, and she was heading out. "Wait," he cried.

She bolted out the door.

"Stop her!" he yelled, but not a soul moved. He tossed the mike to his sister and jumped down from the stage. Shoving and pushing his way past body after body, he finally made it to the steps. Just in time to see Annie's car turn onto Main Street, headed for the interstate.

ANNIE PRESSED on the accelerator and dashed through the yellow light at Main and Fourth. It didn't occur to her until then that Dan could just turn on his flashing lights and follow. She didn't care. She wasn't going to stop until she got to Houston, and he could sound his little siren as loudly as he wanted to.

All her melancholy had evaporated back at the courthouse, replaced instantly by white-hot anger. Did he honestly expect her to stand there after he denied that he'd placed the ad? How many more ways was she supposed to be humiliated? A husband-hunting Barbie thief. That's what they all thought of her. The whole town, right down to the five-year-olds. Oh, wait, scratch that. She was much more famous. She was on the news, on CNN.

She looked in her rearview mirror to see that Dan was keeping a steady pace behind her. All she could do was pray that he didn't have much gas in his tank. She, thank goodness, could make it all the way home.

Why had she gone? What had she been expecting? A miracle? No, she'd just believed Dan. Again. Trusted him to make things right. To rescue her. But all he'd done was confirm that she was a big darn fool.

So, let's see, she thought as she sped up the freeway onramp. *Love life, career, family, reputation. All in the toilet. Pretty impressive for one week's work.* She laughed, because if she didn't, she was going to start crying and never, ever stop.

Dan still trailed close behind, but she didn't want to keep looking at him. That was the failure that mattered most. The one she couldn't laugh off, no matter how much she tried. She could have taken everything else they'd thrown at her, if he'd been by her side. But it was clear to her now that while he wanted her kisses, he didn't want more. He might not think she was a thief, but he also didn't consider her worthy of his love. His vehemence when he denied ever wanting to marry was proof of that. Once that picture hit the papers, the whole town would put two and two together. They'd all know she'd let him into her bed, and that he wasn't there to stay.

Suddenly, her old life wasn't looking so awful. That is, if she had an old life to go back to. What was the administration going to think when they got a load of her on Channel 2? They were not going to be amused. Not by a long shot. So, she probably had failure to get tenure to add to her list of disasters. Not many thieves achieved that lofty goal.

Annie moved into the fast lane and cursed. Really juicy ones. Words she'd never said before, that would have made a sailor blush. It helped, but not enough.

Against her better judgment, she looked in the mirror again. To her surprise, she saw that Dan wasn't alone in his pursuit. Two other police cars were right behind him. At least she thought there were two. That's all she could see.

Great! Now she was officially on the lam. Thelma minus Louise. She shuddered, thinking about how that chase had ended. On the other hand…how far was she from the Grand Canyon?

"Annie, pull over!"

Dan's voice startled her so much the car veered almost all the way onto the shoulder. It was his megaphone, or whatever they called it, of course. But he'd sounded like he was sitting in her back seat.

"Annie, I'm not kidding."

There was only one thing she could think of to let him know exactly how she felt about his suggestion. For the first time in her whole life, she gave an officer of the law a one-fingered salute. It cheered her up immensely.

"Very funny. Now pull over before you get into an accident."

As calmly as a woman going seventy-five miles

per hour could, she turned on her stereo and pushed in the cassette that was sitting by her side. Garth. Good old Garth Brooks. Someone in this world she could always count on.

Surely by the time this side of the tape was over, Dan would give up. He'd have to see that she wasn't going to stop. If he wanted to arrest her, or humiliate her some more, he'd just have to wait until she was in her own home, and even then he'd better bring a whole police force with him, 'cause this girl was not going to go gently.

The irony was that she'd always loved Barbie. She'd had a wonderful collection when she was a girl. Played with them for hours. Dressed them, brushed their hair, seen them off on dates with Ken. Of all the toys or dolls she'd had, Barbie had been the most special. Would she ever be able to see one again without remembering this nightmare? That wasn't fair. Not fair at all.

DAN COULDN'T believe it. His radio had been active for the last ten miles with patrol cars wanting to know who the fugitive was. Last count, ten patrol cars, another sheriff, some Highway Patrol, some police, had joined in on the pursuit. He'd tried to explain that it was Harlen business and he didn't need assistance, but no one wanted to listen.

To make matters worse, half the population of Harlen was in on the chase, too. He'd seen everyone rush to their cars, and now the whole damn freeway was congested. News vans, motorcycles, even two motor homes, all kept up the steady pace. Annie wasn't even breaking the speed limit, so no one was having trouble keeping up.

He should just stop. Go back home. But then Annie would be gone, and thinking he was the biggest stinker this side of New York.

"Annie, please!" he said, his voice echoing back, sounding about as pathetic as he felt. She didn't even glance at him. Well, he wasn't going to give up. Even if it meant leading his entire entourage all the way to her doorstep.

He moved his cruiser up so that he was in the next lane of traffic. His window was down, but hers wasn't. When she finally looked at him, he rolled his hand to mime what he wanted, but she just glared for a moment, then turned back to watch the road.

He ignored his police band as they drove on. He'd catch her eventually. The problem was, what was he going to say to her when he did?

Talk about blowing it. He never should have said that about not wanting a wife. But damn it, the guy had caught him off-guard. And what was this business about a want ad? He smelled a rat by the name of Kirstie in this. His sister had been bugging him to date for so long it had become her mantra. He'd bet money Kirstie was behind this. She was the one who'd introduced him to Annie.

Was Annie under the impression that he'd put that personal ad in there? Jeez. No wonder she thought he was crazy. She'd been expecting Romeo and he'd given her Casanova. Now so much made sense. Her trial run at small-town life was really a test to see if she and he were compatible. She'd come to Harlen because of him!

Lifting the radio to his face once more, he depressed the button and said, "Annie, I didn't know. No one told me about the ad. But Annie, I'm glad."

He knew other people could hear him. Lots of other people. Cops, now from two different counties, were listening in, and every other traveler on the highway with their windows open. He didn't care. Well, not too much. He had to let Annie know that despite his surprise at the town meeting, he was glad she'd come to Harlen, glad she'd been with him, and damn it, he didn't want to lose her.

No. He didn't. Not now, not ever. The realization hit him square in the jaw. He *was* in love with Annie. The thought of being without her for the rest of the summer—for the rest of his life—was unthinkable. She'd done something to him. Changed him. Made him feel again.

"Damn it, Annie, if you don't pull over I *am* going to arrest you. Now, just do it!"

She looked at him again, her expression startled.

"I'm trying to tell you that I love you! You hear me?"

Car horns started blaring behind them. Annie

looked over her shoulder, then quickly back at the road. Instead of slowing to a stop, though, she just sped up. Hadn't she heard him? Or worse, had she heard him, and didn't care?

He wasn't going to wait any longer to find out. He picked up his radio and spoke to his dispatcher.

ANNIE SHOOK as she struggled to keep her attention on the road. Dan loved her? She knew she'd heard him right, but did he mean it?

How could she think when she was being followed by a posse? She couldn't even guess how many cars were back there, but it seemed like hundreds. Police cars with their lights flashing, sirens blaring. The road ahead was almost empty, which made it even worse.

She risked one more look at Dan. When she saw his face, she knew it was over. She had to stop running. One way or the other, she had to know.

16

DAN WAS FAST losing heart. He had to think of some way to get her to believe him, but how? A fifteen-year-old could have handled himself better. He'd bungled with Annie since day one. But she hadn't. She'd tried to tell him back at her apartment that this was big. That they'd turned a corner and discovered something terribly important.

My God, he felt like such a fool. How quickly he'd forgotten that every day before Annie had been hell. That he'd been sour and mean and he'd chased his friends and family away, all because he was an old wounded bear who didn't know how to heal. But since Annie...

Since Annie, he'd laughed again. He'd looked forward to his days. His nights. Work was work again, and not the only place on earth he felt a little useful.

The curse of his marriage had been lifted by a woman whose only sin was that she'd come to town at his request—only he hadn't known it at the time. She'd walked into a crazy world where Barbies were stolen and Harlen made the national news and everyone in town was playing detective. He didn't know why it had to be so mixed-up, but then, there were a lot of mysteries he couldn't solve. Annie herself was one. But that investigation was worthy of a lifetime of effort.

He looked at her again, and he smiled. Miracle of miracles, she smiled back. It was a tentative grin, but it was something. Then she gestured for him to move back.

It could be a trick. He could slow down, and then she could shoot off again and try to lose him, but with half the state of Texas following them, he doubted she'd get far. He just nodded, and eased his foot off the accelerator.

Sure enough, Annie changed lanes and began to slow down. Bright girl, she took her time, giving everyone in back of them a chance to hit the brakes safely. Finally, though, she was on the right shoulder, and he came up behind her and put his cruiser in park.

She'd ended up next to a wide field, and soon it began to look like an auto rally, what with the police cars, the sedans and the motor homes filling up every available foot. No one, it seemed, wanted to miss this. Dan thought about taking out his rifle and ordering them all to head back home, but even that probably wouldn't make them listen.

When he got out of his car, the first person he noticed was Kirstie. She was running toward him with Reese right behind her. Frank and Ted were shaggin' it too. He wondered where his mother was.

He didn't know about the rest of them, but he certainly wanted to talk to his sister. But that would have to wait. Annie was still in her car.

He approached her carefully, wanting to give himself a little time to figure out what to say. The closer he got, the harder it was not to break into a run. He wanted her so much. He wanted to see her face so he'd know for sure that he was right. That she did love him, and that she knew he loved her back.

She'd rolled down her window. It wasn't enough. He opened the door for her and held out his hand. She took it, looking up at him, then let him help her out.

By the time she stood in front of him, the crowd, which now included police, reporters, most of the women who'd had Barbies stolen, and his family, surrounded them. Dan didn't give them more than a cursory look and a scowl before his attention returned to Annie.

"Are you going to arrest me?" she asked softly.

Camera lights went on, and Dan moved closer to Annie. "No. That's not why I came after you."

"I didn't come to Harlen to trick you into marrying me or anything," she said. "I didn't know the ad wasn't real. Actually, it was Rachel who made me come. I didn't even think I was going to like you."

He smiled. "Well, then, we both got tricked,

huh? I believe my sister has some explaining to do."

"Hey, wait a minute," someone yelled, and Dan spun around to see the photographer that had ambushed them in the hallway. "How come you're not arresting her? Is it because you're sleeping with her?"

Cameras clicked furiously, and Dan reached for Annie's hand. "I'm not arresting her because she's not guilty."

"How do we know that? Didn't you find a shoe at her apartment?"

"A planted shoe, yes. I'm telling you, she's not guilty."

"Well, if you won't arrest her, there are plenty of cops here who can."

Dan moved until his body blocked Annie from the onlookers. "Whoever wants to try is welcome, but they'll have to get through me, first."

The crowd before them jostled, and then Kirstie and the rest of his family moved right beside Dan.

"Kirstie has something to tell you," Reese said.

"You were in on it, too!" She looked around, guilt making her pretty eyes wide. "You all were. Remember? Don't make me the villain."

"She's right, Dan," Margaret Albright said. "We all volunteered."

"Everyone got behind this one, Danny boy," Frank said. "Even Mom."

"It's just that you were so miserable," Kirstie said.

"And making us miserable right along with you," Reese added, to the crowd's amusement.

"So the whole lot of you got together and put an ad in a magazine?"

"It was a real nice ad, Dan."

Several people agreed.

Kirstie nodded. "There's more."

The look on her face didn't bode well. She looked awfully young, suddenly, and a little frightened.

"Out with it."

"We'd better show you, right, Reese?"

He nodded. Dan took Annie's hand, and followed his siblings to Reese's Lincoln Continental. To the back end, actually. Reese got his keys out and popped the trunk.

Dan's jaw dropped. Boxes of Barbies were neatly lined up and stacked. He recognized the Pink Jubilee, Hair Happening redhead, the Color Magic and the American Girl. And those were just the ones on top. His gaze moved to Annie, who appeared as dumbfounded as himself, then to Reese. "You're the Barbie thief?"

Reese chuckled. "Not exactly."

"Then how...?"

"Dan, Annie, first let me say that our intentions were good. None of us realized it could get this out of hand."

"What's going on?" someone yelled from the back.

"The mayor has all the stolen Barbies in the trunk!" a man shouted.

"He getting arrested?"

"Nope. Not yet."

Dan tried to ignore the cameras, the shouting, the jostling, and just understand what was happening. "What do you mean, your intentions were good?"

"Well," Kirstie said, not meeting his eyes, "you wouldn't go out on a date. You certainly wouldn't voluntarily put your own ad in *Texas Men*. But we all knew you'd follow a suspect."

"You mean, everyone knew I wasn't guilty?" Annie asked. "It was all a setup?"

Kirstie nodded. "It just, well, the story broke, and it never occurred to me that the national services would pick it up. But we could all tell that you two were falling in love, so no one wanted to botch that up in the middle."

"I don't believe this," Dan said. "Are you people crazy?"

"Hey, what kind of a scam is this?" It was the reporter for the Houston station. "Are you telling me that there never were any stolen Barbies? That this is a hoax?"

Kirstie turned to her colleagues. "I wouldn't exactly call it a hoax."

"Then what would you call it?"

She turned to look at Dan and Annie. "Matchmaking!"

Laughter moved in waves as the little joke

spread to the outlying folks. The reporters, however, didn't seem amused.

"I told you that there was no story," Kirstie said. "You wouldn't listen."

"You made me waste four days in that Podunk town of yours for nothing?" the CNN man said.

"Not for nothing," Kirstie said. "It's a great human-interest story. I'll be happy to fill in all the details when we get back to Harlen. I mean, how often does Barbie help two people fall in love? Or get a whole town to play matchmaker? You've got to admit, it's a heck of a story."

The CNN man grumbled, but he instructed his photographer to take more pictures of Kirstie, Reese, the dolls and of course the happy couple.

Dan still felt stunned, as if he was missing an important piece of information. He turned to Annie and took both her hands in his. "I don't know how to apologize for this. If I'd had even the slightest notion these wackos were setting us up, I'd have run them all into jail."

"I see. I think." Annie shook her head. "Everyone knew? They don't all hate me?"

"Hate you?" Kirstie said. "We knew from the first day that you were the right woman for Dan. Honey, we're all behind you a hundred percent."

"But why didn't you tell me?"

Kirstie shrugged. "Rachel said not to."

"*She's* in on this?"

Reese nodded. "She thought she'd better come out here and talk to you. She's on her way now."

"So she isn't missing? She never was working for that attorney?"

"No, she is. But he's a nice guy, and he gave her a few days off."

"I'm sorry. I just can't believe any of this. Why you all went to such trouble."

"Because we love Dan. And we want him to be happy." Ted Collins came up to Annie and kissed her on the cheek. "You make him happy, Annie." He turned to Dan. "Isn't that right, little brother?"

Dan wasn't sure what he was supposed to feel. Angry? Relieved? Foolish? But then he looked at Annie, and relief won. "He's right. I don't agree with the way they did this. Not by a long shot. But..."

"It worked, didn't it?" Jessie Higgins cried out. "He loves her! I knew he would."

"Oh, come on, Jess," Gina Painter said. "Just yesterday you said it was a crackpot idea."

"I did not. I could see he was moony over her from the second day."

"It don't matter what you two think," a highway-patrol cop said. "What matters is what this here couple thinks."

All gazes were on Dan and Annie now and, despite being just off the highway in a big old field filled with vehicles parked back to back, a hush settled over the crowd like fog in the morning. Everyone waited for Dan to say something. Especially the woman in front of him.

"So, uh, what was it about that ad that you

liked?" he said, trying to keep the conversation just between the two of them.

"Dan asked her what it was in the ad she liked!" Margaret shouted. So much for privacy.

"What'd she say?" someone from the left cried.

"Hold on. She hasn't answered yet!"

Dan shook his head. "I can try and arrest them all, but I don't think meddling is even a misdemeanor."

"It's too late," Annie said. "It seems to me that ship has sailed."

He grinned. "With everyone on board."

"I guess we can just ignore them."

"Annie says she can just ignore us!" Margaret yelled.

Laughter broke out in the ranks. "Not likely," Reese said.

Dan focused on Annie, determined not to be sidetracked again. "Well?"

"Your picture was nice," she said. "And I liked that you seemed to love living in your small town so much." She smiled shyly. "Would you like to know what it said?"

"You remember?"

"Every word. 'Single Sheriff Seeks...' That's how it started."

"Then what?"

"It said, 'Hi, I'm Dan Collins. I'm the sheriff here in Harlen, Texas, a little town just outside of Houston.' But that wasn't the good part."

"What was?"

"It said, 'Pretty isn't as important as nice.'"

"You're the prettiest thing I've ever seen."

"Thanks. But I didn't need to be."

"No. I would have fallen for you no matter what you looked like."

"I believe you. It also said the women who answered the ad should like the pace of small-town living."

"Now you know the truth about that. I would think you'd never want to go back to Harlen again. Not after what they did to you."

"I admit, it was the oddest welcome I imagine any person's ever gotten. But I do appreciate that your friends care about you so much, they'd go to all this trouble."

"I think they were just bored and needed to stir things up a little."

"No. This was personal. They did it for you."

"So what should I tell them? Did the plan work?"

Annie stared into Dan's big brown eyes for a long time. She forgot where she was and that everyone was watching. She blocked out the sounds of the traffic and the click of flashbulbs. Her whole attention was on only one thing—seeing what was in Dan Collins's gaze and in his heart.

What she saw made her swallow hard. There was a little trepidation, but only a little. Mostly what she saw was hope, and love, and the sweet gentleness that had drawn her to him from the first. It had worked. For both of them. Despite everything. Or maybe, because of everything. She had fallen, at long last, in love with a man, a crazy town, a new job.... But mostly the man.

"It worked," she whispered.

"It worked!" Margaret yelled.

A whoop went up from the crowd, and the hollering just got louder when Dan leaned over and took her in his arms. When he kissed her, the noise level sounded like the last game of the World Series.

Finally, after Dan and Annie had been congratulated, slapped on the back, photographed, and teased by practically every man, woman and child in the field, things settled down. Folks started heading back to their cars. The police lights went out. Even the reporters packed it in.

But before Annie got into her car, she saw a big rig slow down to the side of the road. The driver leaned out and yelled, "What's this? An accident?"

"No," Margaret yelled right back at him. "We planned the whole damn thing!"

Annie laughed and turned to Dan. His smile was the most wonderful thing she'd ever seen. "You think one of the kind folks from Harlen could drive my car back? I think I'd like to ride back with you."

He nodded. "I was thinking the same thing. But I warn you. That'll mean you're under house arrest. The sentence is life."

She held out her hands, wrists together. "Take me in, Officer."

"Yes, ma'am," he said. "Yes, ma'am."

Epilogue

ANNIE RAN her hand over her belly, hardly believing the time had finally arrived. She felt incredibly calm, but that was probably because Dan was a wreck. He'd come the moment she'd called, his siren blaring all the way down Main Street. Now he was running around like a madman, even though they'd had the bag packed for two weeks, and the hospital wasn't more than ten minutes away.

"I'll be right back," he said. "Let me just take this to the car."

"Dan? I don't think I'll need my coat."

"What?" He looked down and saw that he'd picked up her winter coat along with the suitcase. "Oh, yeah." He tossed it over the big chair and promptly tripped over Cougar.

"Maybe I'd better walk down with you," she said.

"No! No, I'll be back. You just breathe."

"I'll be fine, I promise." She walked, or rather waddled, over to her husband and took him by the hand. "Come on, honey. We've got plenty of time."

Dan grasped her hand, then let it go when he

got to the door. He kept his gaze on her as if she was going to bolt, which was sort of laughable given her condition. But she let it go. She knew it was because he was so concerned. But she also knew that the delivery was going to go without a hitch. How? She didn't even question it. She just knew.

Dan walked by her side to the elevator, then let her get in first. He hit the button and tapped his fingers on his thigh the whole way down.

"What are you thinking?" she asked, seeing the fierce look of concentration on his face.

"Breathing. We're not breathing right. I can't remember anything from those classes, Annie. Nothing."

"Don't worry. We'll figure it out."

"I'm gonna blow it."

"Fortunately, you're not the one that has to do the important work today."

He took in a deep breath. "I just want to make you comfortable."

"And you'll do great."

The elevator stopped, and Dan put his hand on the center of her back as they walked to the truck. It didn't seem to matter that she was an old married lady of almost two years. His touch still thrilled her.

He raced to the passenger door and opened it for her, ready with his hands and his strength to help her in. Once she was seated, another contraction hit, and she concentrated on letting go, on re-laxing.

"Damn!" Dan raced around and got behind the wheel. The whole way over to the hospital, he kept asking her if she was okay, until she didn't know whether to laugh or cry.

But they made it. And faster than she could have imagined, she was in her room and the doctor had finished his examination. Her contractions were pretty steady now, and in a moment, they were going to wheel her to the delivery room.

Dan's hand held on to hers tightly. She was scared, but excited. Pretty soon, their little girl was going to come into the world. They were going to be a real family. Parents. The best parents in the world, because they had so much love between them, and so much love to give.

"How's she doing, Dan?"

Dan turned toward the voice at the door. "Soon, Margaret. Real soon."

"Everyone's rooting for you. Kirstie and Reese are on their way. So is Rachel. Your mom is coming in, too, Dan."

"Thanks."

"And the guys from the station are all rooting for you."

"Great."

"Oh, and Channel Two wants to do a follow-up story."

"No!" Dan said.

"No!" Annie said, at the exact same moment.

"But they've been following you two since the beginning!"

"Margaret, you just tell them they can find another story. We have work to do here."

"All right. But can't I even tell them..."

"No!"

Margaret grumbled, but she left. Annie didn't care anymore. She was too busy. The baby was coming. She grabbed Dan's hand and found his gaze. "She's here," she said.

Dan pounced on the nurses' button, and then it was rushing and pain and yelling and lights and breathing until Annie couldn't think of anything but having the child.

"One more push, honey."

She grabbed on tight and pushed with everything she had in her. A moment later, blessed relief, and an even more blessed cry. Her daughter was here. Finally.

"She's perfect," the doctor said.

Dan leaned down, tears streaming, and kissed her. "*You're* perfect."

"Can I hold her?"

"Of course, Mom," the doctor said. And then he laid her brand-new baby on her tummy. So beautiful. So pink and healthy. So incredible.

"Daddy?" she whispered to Dan. "I think there's someone here who wants to meet you."

"Yeah?"

"Uh-huh."

He held his finger out and touched the child's hand. Instantly, the little one gripped it tight.

"Daddy," Annie said. "Meet Barbie."

Take 2 bestselling love stories FREE

Plus get a FREE surprise gift!

Special Limited-Time Offer

Mail to Harlequin Reader Service®

> 3010 Walden Avenue
> P.O. Box 1867
> Buffalo, N.Y. 14240-1867

YES! Please send me 2 free Harlequin Temptation® novels and my free surprise gift. Then send me 4 brand-new novels every month, which I will receive before they appear in bookstores. Bill me at the low price of $3.12 each plus 25¢ delivery and applicable sales tax, if any.* That's the complete price, and a saving of over 10% off the cover prices—quite a bargain! I understand that accepting the books and gift places me under no obligation ever to buy any books. I can always return a shipment and cancel at any time. Even if I never buy another book from Harlequin, the 2 free books and the surprise gift are mine to keep forever.

142 HEN CH7G

Name	(PLEASE PRINT)	
Address	Apt. No.	
City	State	Zip

This offer is limited to one order per household and not valid to present Harlequin Temptation® subscribers. *Terms and prices are subject to change without notice. Sales tax applicable in N.Y.

HARLEQUIN®

Temptation®

*He's strong. He's sexy.
He's up for grabs!*

Harlequin Temptation and
Texas Men magazine present:

1998 Mail Order Men

#691 THE LONE WOLF
by Sandy Steen—July 1998

#695 SINGLE IN THE SADDLE
by Vicki Lewis Thompson—August 1998

#699 SINGLE SHERIFF SEEKS...
by Jo Leigh—September 1998

#703 STILL HITCHED, COWBOY
by Leandra Logan—October 1998

#707 TALL, DARK AND RECKLESS
by Lyn Ellis—November 1998

#711 MR. DECEMBER
by Heather MacAllister—December 1998

*Mail Order Men—
Satisfaction Guaranteed!*

Available wherever Harlequin books are sold.

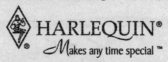

HARLEQUIN®

Makes any time special ™

Welcome to
THE COWBOY CLUB

It's a place where romance and the West come together.... And legend says any man and woman who meet here will get hitched before the year is out!

Meet Clay McCormick. This lean, sexy cowboy is full of heartache. Can gorgeous Erica Ross ease his pain, when she's got secrets of her own?

Come on down to
THE COWBOY CLUB
and look for—

#702 *Love You Forever*
(October 1998)

#714 *The Bride Wore Boots*
(January 1999)

Two dynamic books by popular
Janice Kaiser!

Available at your favorite retail outlet.

 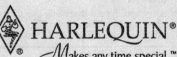

COMING NEXT MONTH

#701 IN HOT PURSUIT Patricia Ryan
Hero for Hire

Of all the bodyguard assignments Roman Fitzpatrick had endured, this was the hardest. He had to protect Summer Love; she didn't want protection. He blamed gossip-hungry journalists for destroying his police career; she was a flighty gossip columnist. He was a man; she was a woman....

#702 LOVE YOU FOREVER Janice Kaiser
The Cowboy Club

The moment Erica Ross walked into the Cowboy Club her life changed. The legendary Western place oozed romance and cowboys. And tall, sexy, strapping Clay McCormick was exactly the kind of man she needed. But could it last *forever*?

#703 STILL HITCHED, COWBOY Leandra Logan
Mail Order Men

Matt Colter advertised for the woman of his dreams in *Texas Men* magazine. What he got was a nightmare! A blond socialite fiancée, Tiffany—and a beautiful brunette ex-wife, Jenna, who wasn't *exactly* an ex. This cowboy was still hitched, still in love...and he had to follow his heart!

#704 A TOUCH OF BLACK VELVET Carrie Alexander
Blaze

Alec Danielli *knew* that being Lacey Longwood's protector would sorely test him. She was the Black Velvet vixen, Madame X—*every* man's fantasy. And he couldn't touch her....

AVAILABLE NOW: